MESSENGERS IN WHITE

Borgo Press Books by Ardath Mayhar

The Absolutely Perfect Horse: A Young Adult Novel (with Marylois Dunn)
The Body in the Swamp: An Occult Mystery
Carrots and Miggle: A Novel of East Texas
The Clarrington Heritage
Closely Knit in Scarlatt
Crazy Quilt: The Best Short Stories of Ardath Mayhar
Deadly Memoir
Death in the Square
The Door in the Hill: A Tale of the Turnipins
The Dropouts: A Tale of Growing Up in East Texas
Feud at Sweetwater Creek: A Novel of the Old West
The Fugitives: A Tale of Prehistoric Times
The Heirs of Three Oaks: A Novel of the Old West
High Mountain Winter: A Novel of the Old West
How the Gods Wove in Kyrannon: Tales of the Triple Moons
Hunters of the Plains: A Novel of Prehistoric America
Island in the Lake: A Novel of Native America
Khi to Freedom: A Science Fiction Novel
The Lintons of Skillet Bend: A Novel of East Texas
Lone Runner: A Novel of the Old West
Lords of the Triple Moons: A Science Fantasy Novel: Tales of the Triple Moons
Makra Choria: A Novel of High Fantasy
Medicine Dream: Being the Further Adventures of Burr Henderson
Messengers in White: A Science Fantasy Novel
Monkey Station: A Novel of the Future (Macaque Cycle #1; with Ron Fortier)
People of the Mesa: A Novel of Native America
A Planet Called Heaven: A Science Fiction Novel
Prescription for Danger: A Novel of the Old West
Reflections; & Journey to an Ending: Collected Poems
A Road of Stars: A Fantasy of Life, Death, Love, and Art
Runes of the Lyre: A Science Fantasy Novel
The Saga of Grittel Sundotha: A Science Fantasy Novel
The Seekers of Shar-Nuhn: Tales of the Triple Moons
Shock Treatment: An Account of Granary's War
Slewfoot Sally and the Flying Mule: Tall Tales from Cotton County, Texas
Soul-Singer of Tyrnos: A Fantasy Novel
Strange Doings in the Pine Hills: Stories
Through a Stone Wall: Lessons from Thirty Years of Writing
Timber Pirates: A Novel of East Texas (with Marylois Dunn)
Towers of the Earth: A Novel of Native America
Trail of the Seahawks: A Novel of the Future (Macaque Cycle #2; with R. Fortier)
The Tulpa: A Novel of Fantasy
Two-Moons and the Black Tower: A Novel of Fantasy
Vendetta
Warlock's Gift: Tales of the Triple Moons
The World Ends in Hickory Hollow: A Novel of the Future
A World of Weirdities: Tales to Shiver By

MESSENGERS IN WHITE

A SCIENCE FANTASY NOVEL

by

Ardath Mayhar

THE BORGO PRESS

An Imprint of Wildside Press LLC

MMIX

CONTENTS

ABOUT THE AUTHOR

The author of sixty-two books, more than forty of them published commercially, ARDATH MAYHAR began her career in the early eighties with science fiction novels from Doubleday and TSR. Atheneum published several of her young adult and children's novels. Changing focus, she wrote westerns (as **Frank Cannon**) and mountain man novels (as **John Killdeer**), four prehistoric Indian books under her own name, and historical western *High Mountain Winter* under the byline **Frances Hurst**.

Recently she has been working with on-line publishers. *A Road of Stars* was her first original novel to appear in print-on-demand format. Many of her out-of-print titles are now available from e-publishers fictionwise.com and renebooks.com; many other novels are being published by the Borgo Press Imprint of Wildside Press and Amazon.com.

Now in her seventies, Mayhar was widowed in 1999, after forty-one years of marriage, and has four grown sons. She now works at home, writing short fiction and nonfiction, and doing book doctoring professionally. Her web pages can be found at:

w2.netdot.com/ardathm/ and
http://ofearna.us/ books/mayhar.html

FOREWORD

This tale, more perhaps than any other I have written, reflects my attitude toward gender-based roles. Having been reared to be a fully functional human being, ready to tackle any task at hand, whether or not it suited my size, I have proven for myself that I can do just about anything.

Over more than seven decades of observation, I have seen that those who fear strong women who have wisdom do so because they know themselves to be both weak and unwise, whether the fearful be male or female. The patriarchal teachings are a defense against those whom males fear, and those of radical feminism reveal a similar fear of being victimized by men. Yet one allows oneself to be a victim, through fear or ignorance or carefully instilled guilt. Too often, parents teach their offspring these destructive beliefs.

If we talked less and thought more, refrained from training our children to respect as strong those who are merely violent, it might be that we could create a world in which no one would need to control or enslave anyone else.

—Ardath Mayhar
Chireno, Texas
October 2007

PROLOGUE

COMMAND CODE Number 2-J-R #$$ 6

Deposited upon planet C-136 (called Halash): 500 colonization specialists, with genetic material for propagating human, animal, and vegetable species.

Sealed deposits of emergency weaponry. Training program for custodians. Suitable tools, clothing, impermanent shelter components.

DIRECTIVE:

Colonize planet, in self sustaining mode, for eventual movement further into adjacent arm of galaxy, according to Pan-Galactic policy.

PRESENT STATUS:

Completed.
No further contact necessary.

CHAPTER ONE

The weight of the sleeping child was heavy and warm against Lehnik's chest. The round head nodded into the crook of his arm as they moved together to the slow gait of the horse as it picked its careful way up the steep trail. The soldier found the feel of the small body pleasant.

He had never been so close to a small one before. Even his brothers had not been younger than he but older, and he had never been near his young nieces and nephews. This responsibility had been thrust upon him unexpectedly, and he found it less of a burden than he had thought.

The child was serious, with grave good manners for one so young. It was hard to believe that she could count only three years of life. He felt pity for her dead mother. She must have been an unusual woman to rear such a contained and controlled daughter.

Lehnik closed his eyes for a moment, fighting sleep, but his head drooped almost to the fur cap that topped the child's fine fair hair. He jerked awake and found that his mount had paused before a thick log lying athwart the trail that crooked at this point around a hairpin curve.

Lehnik looked about, squinting to see through the light snow that now fell through the dimness of late afternoon. This was no accidental deadfall. The log had been cut to fit exactly into its niche, and it met the sheer stone of the cliff wall at his right with neat precision. That meant, he assumed, that he was supposed to dismount here. One approached the House of the Silent Women on foot, he had been told when Krohm, his commander, sent him on this mission.

He shifted the sleeping weight of the child onto his shoulder and flung a leg over the saddle pad in order to slip to the ground. Small Cylla murmured something but did not wake as he huddled his cloak about both of them and turned to climb over the log. As he stepped high, a bright-shafted arrow thunked into the wood beside his knee.

He froze, foot aloft, with an icy sweat starting between his shoulder blades. He cleared his throat twice before he could find his voice. "Lehnik Avarien, Master of Horse, comes with an orphaned child to place in the care of the Sisters of Silence. I beg your permission to continue, for the child is very young and the snow is growing worse."

There was no reply, and Lehnik had expected none. He had been told more than once, in tale-telling sessions between campaigns, that the Sisters allowed their tongues to be removed after taking their strange oath of fidelity and honor. Yet in his wandering about the lands he had sat more than once in an inn while a pair of the white-clad women ate at a nearby table. He was certain that they did have tongues to manage their food with, though they had never been heard to utter more than a grunt of appreciation for good service.

He had found their silence pleasant. Most women's chatter was sharp-tongued, whether they were farm mistresses or instructors-at-arms, herbalists or beekeepers. Many of the women he had met as the army traveled talked fit to pierce the brain, their voices shrill and constant.

In these days of war, Trans-Kell was served and operated principally by women who had watched their men ride away to do battle with contentious neighbors or raiding bandits. They seemed not to mind it all that much, but did the hard work with gusto and skill.

He had heard one brawny smith say to a farm-wife whose horse she was shoeing, "A man is a comfort on a cold night, but he isn't really necessary in the business." She had looked capable of dealing with any task life might bring her, too.

He understood that other countries had other ways, and there were places on Halash where women were treated as chattels. Trans-Kell was not so ignorant and used every resource available.

It had made him wonder, at times, why the House of Silent Women never lacked for applicants. Women had no need to flee from domineering husbands or fathers. The reverse was more nearly true. What precious thing did this remote retreat offer its members?

He found himself hurrying up the steep path that climbed the mountain, afire to see what might lie at its top. But another arrow chunked solidly into a tree at his right. He stopped again and waited. This had to be another checkpoint. Another figure, almost invisible in its white cloak amid the snow, wavered toward him. His heart thumped hard before it steadied as a short, stocky shape paused beside him, inspecting him closely. Her eyes were almost hidden in the folds of a white woolen head cloth, and her hand rose to point toward the left. It had seemed to Lehnik that only a sheer drop lay in that direction.

But he was no coward. Besides, he knew the woman had seen the child on his shoulder, so he moved cautiously, feeling ahead with each foot before trusting his weight to it. Each time there was a foothold ahead, seemingly cut into the stone face of the mountain. The path slanted inward, toward the cliff, so that its slick surface might not send a walker skittering over the edge.

He followed his guide for a long time. In that cut between mountain peaks it was dark, now, and he slowed still more, holding the child carefully close to his right shoulder.

Then he stopped short and called to the one he followed, "My horse! It's cold and hungry and weary! Will someone care for him?"

The woman's hand moved, and though he did not actually interpret her motions, he felt reassured. Almost as clearly as if she had spoken, he understood that someone would lead his mount to shelter and tend its needs. Lehnik sighed with relief as they began to climb again.

The track now inched upward along what might have been a deep cleft across the top of the mountain, if he could have seen it clearly. It grew steeper, and he could see a faint glimmer above him, as if a lamp were shining through the snow. Now he stepped with more assurance, for the drop was no longer beside the path, and soon his head rose above the lip of the cut and he moved into a formal garden, which was buried in a thick blanket of white.

Ignoring the snow, he stood for a long moment, staring. A circle of stone benches held fat cushions of snow and enclosed a fountain that had been carved into the shape of a cat. The water that must spout from its mouth in summer was now a trickle of icicles that dripped from its marble whiskers.

Dark conifers rimmed the spot, and skeletons of ornamental shrubs hinted at flower stalks. Even in the chill black and white of the night and the snow, it held a strange sort of peace.

The woman touched his fur-cloaked shoulder, and Lehnik came to himself. Now he turned to follow his guide—or guard, perhaps—with a word of apology on his lips. She nodded as she pushed through a bank of glossy-leaved shrubs and held them aside so that he could pass without having the twigs brush the child he held. Tiny orange berries glowed among the leaves, seeming to hold the lamplight that revealed them. One dropped into the snow at his foot as he passed, and he thought that it seemed bright and ominous, like a drop of blood.

Ahead he could see a tall doorway, its arch crowned with a plumed keystone, the lintel delicately carved. The guide knocked sharply, and it swung wide, letting a warm breath of scented air out into the cold night. Lehnik almost staggered, as he entered the room, for the contrast with the outdoor was stunning. He could see no fire, but the very walls seemed to emit heat.

The sounds of voices—many voices of children—came from a room beyond a door that was curtained with crimson. A hand pushed the curtain aside, and an ample woman in a damp apron came into the room and stood looking quizzically at Lehnik and his burden.

"Ah, another waif, is it? Orphaned, I have no doubt, and brought here to be reared by the Sisters. Let me take it. A boy or a girl?" Her voice was deep and gruff and, he thought, infinitely kind.

Her question shocked him. He understood at once that, whoever she might be, she was not one of the silent Sisters.

"A girl," he replied. "Her name is Cylla, and her mother was Master of Orkell Farmstead in Dreit. Her father is dead, killed fighting bandits. Her mother died in the raid across Kell-ford a week ago."

He found himself staring at the woman. Though she asked sharp questions, she had a motherly air, and he suspected that she must be the matron in charge of the children brought here for nurture. He wondered how those who demanded silence could bear her babble, however, for now she ran on with commiserations for the child, questions shot at him, and comments on the tragedy of the wars and the raiding Ellain.

But she was interrupted by his guide, who led him away to an alcove in a corridor that led from the entry-room that held the outer door. There she gestured for him to bend his head and close his eyes. He had been a warrior for too long to feel comfortable about doing that, but he swallowed and obeyed. She bound a long scarf firmly about his eyes.

He could tell by the echoes of his steps that they entered the corridor again. He smelled damp marble, cut granite, and then fresh-cut greenery. He moved blindly until he was brought up by a touch on his arm.

There came a grating sound, and damp air gushed into his face. A solid hand took his and led him down many shallow steps, across a long flat space, and up another flight of steps. The smell of water on stone mingled with that of fungus. The air was still warm and humid.

He had long since lost his bearings when she led him through another doorway, which he knew because his elbow brushed the side of it, and along another echoing corridor. Then she halted him and removed the blindfold. He stared around, blinded by the intense light reflected from white stone. The walls and the floor were dazzling, and a single column curved gracefully to hold the arch of a stair that spiraled upward.

The woman pointed. He must go there, upward yet again. He had all but given up hope of reaching anyone who was empowered with speech, by the time they had wandered up more corridors and climbed even more stairs. At last, in a silent white hallway, he was startled by a breath of moving air in the stillness.

His warrior instinct carried him against a wall, his blade leaping into his hand by reflex, as white-clad woman swirled out of a door ahead and attacked him in what seemed an earnest attempt to kill him. As he parried desperately, a strange mood seized him. Automatically, almost in a fog, he fought for his life.

He flicked aside her thrusting blade, but others appeared as more white shapes moved in the corridor. More and more intensely, he dealt with swords that sought to pierce his vitals, and the hall clanged with metal kissing metal. Lehnik felt almost disembodied, caught in a nightmare battle that seemed to have no end. Even if he died, he wondered if it would stop or if he might not continue it into whatever life might come next.

The warmth leached out of the air, and his lungs, burning at first, now burned with the chill, as well. Suddenly he was so cold that he could hardly move, his blood seeming to congeal as his adversaries dwindled and he faced a single one at last, a woman and not a mist of shining steel.

He found himself standing, frozen, his blade trapped in mid-air, his feet locked in a sidestep. Whispers echoed in his head, thoughts not his own, blurred and distorted. He thought that he caught the words, "...moves well...," in a murmur. "Warrior," another asserted. Neither was a voice, but both seemed the shadows of whispers.

It was as if thoughts moved about him, and he was able to catch only a very few of the strongest, as they passed from mind to mind.

Strong hands grabbed him by the elbows and bore him through sterile white corridors to set him down at last in a room that was

13

bursting with light. Not white light, this time, but warm yellow light seemed to glow from the marble.

Now the air was warm again, and his hands tingled with the sensation of returning circulation. His feet relaxed from that interrupted step, and he felt as if he might be a statue that had been granted the gift of life.

The room seemed empty; only a pale golden pillar stood in its center, holding a basin and ewer. Beyond it a door opened, and Lehnik stared as he had never stared before. Through the door came a woman who was draped in fabric so white that it seemed woven of light. Or was it merely that her skin was so intensely black the robe was a startling contrast? Her eyes gleamed above her lowered face veil, a liquid darkness in a polished face whose beauty stunned him.

She moved, and her grace woke a pang in his loins, yet he was gently bred and he made no sign. He merely moved his arm to remove its stiffness and repositioned his feet as they tingled and burned with returning life. When she approached, he bent his neck, as to a person of power and authority.

"So you are Lehnik Avarien," she said. Her voice was lined with velvet.

The fact that she spoke at all startled him. "I thought...that your sisterhood were forbidden to speak," he said.

She chuckled, a rich ripple of sound in the bright room. "That would lead to a great deal of misunderstanding with our fellows in Trans-Kell," she said. "One of our order is always appointed Speaker for the House of Silence, and I am she. When there is need, I go out as emissary to governments not only of this country but of our neighbors. And when we have a visitor, I am the one who greets him."

He considered asking a very impertinent question. Then, deciding to risk it, he said, "What just happened out in the corridor? Did those women really intend to kill me?"

This time she laughed aloud. "If they had so intended, Lehnik, you would be dead. They are trained for that. No, our rule is that all who come must be tested, for it becomes tiring, only trying your skills against familiar opponents. New skills, unfamiliar techniques are relished here." Her great black eyes gleamed with humor.

"You gave them good sport, and they approve of you. You might like to see...yes, I believe you would. Too many are not interested in what we do here, but you may look into the ewer, if you wish."

14

Lehnik found himself moving toward the low pillar to stare down into the pitcher of clear water. His breath rippled it into tiny waves, and then it smoothed, and he saw....

A summer forest. Half hidden in the undergrowth were children, some very young, some older, and all were armed with bows or blades measured to their sizes. Silently, as he watched, they laid an ambush. A pair of Sisters, who were coming along a path through the trees, were surprised by their small attackers, and all fought a silent battle there in the shadows.

Lehnik recognized the determined ferocity of that engagement. He saw no blood, but there was a great deal of skill and energy.

The water rippled again, and when it cleared once more he saw a young girl walking down a corridor that he recognized as one he had just traversed. Three veiled and robed shapes broke from the cover of three doorways and converged upon her. She caught up one of the small statues from its pedestal and beat them away with it until she gained the foot of the stair.

Once at its top she heaved the white stone figure down upon her attackers, knocking one to the floor. Two heavy jars from the stair-head followed it, bowling over the other two Sisters. Then all three rose to their feet and ran up to embrace the girl, who was flushed and triumphant.

Again the water moved and cleared. Lehnik looked into a magnificent chamber, where at a long table were seated men and women whose faces reflected maturity and wisdom. The woman's voice murmured into his ear, "This is the Ruling Council of Trans-Kell. Of those twenty people, fourteen were taught here on this mountaintop.

"That is why we are able to hold our contentious neighbors from sacking our towns. It is the reason why this nation fights no wars of conquest. For here those rulers learned the greatest of disciplines, which is that of the self. They have no space for greed in their spirits."

Lehnik looked up from the water into her eyes. "I see. I had wondered, through the years, how that came to be, considering that most of those I know who would like to join that council lusted after power. It puzzled me how the ones holding the seats were so far superior to those who would like to hold them." He frowned, remembering.

"Yet I have heard it said that your Sisterhood commits...forbidden practices."

She frowned in turn. "Women lying with women? That happens even in the countryside below us. But it is an old canard, used by

15

those too dimwitted to think of anything else to our discredit. It is laughable, for those who have the control to give up even their power of speech find it possible to give up carnal lusts, as well. They commit those energies to more important matters.

"We work at learning or art or crafts, at fine weaponry and the strategies of war, as skill and inclinations lead us. We burn the spirits of our people clean, here on this mountain, and not all of the sisters are women, you will find." She laughed again at his astonishment.

Lehnik thought back to all the Sisters he had met in his military career. They were so swaddled in white robes and veils that no one could say truly what sort of body lay beneath. As they never spoke, their voices could not betray them. They wore gloves, always, which concealed their hands.

He had seen for himself they understood techniques of warfare that had turned the tide of more than one battle. They were so skilled at personal combat that none challenged any of their number more than once. It was quite possible that he had traveled beside more than one male Sister in his time.

"Then it is not forbidden for a man to become one of your number," he mused. He thought of his long years of forays and engagements. He recalled the child he had brought across all those dangerous miles and the strange feeling of warmth that filled him when he thought of her.

He glanced up into the Sister's dark eyes. "Do none of those male and female Sisters ever find a life companion among their own number?"

"They do. Then they become lay Sisters and move lower on the mountain to till the fields or man the tanneries and weapon shops and other matters that must serve any community. It is their children, principally, who are taught in our school, though of late we have placed many orphans among them."

Lehnik touched his sword, again hanging at his belt. His hand lingered on its worn hilt as he shifted his feet and moved his shoulders, feeling his old tunic strain. He threw back his fur cape, for an unusual warmth was coursing through his body. He felt he was about to be freed from some old servitude.

"Would you consider admitting me?" he asked, his tone diffident.

She bent her long neck in a nod. "It was agreed among us that you would be a welcome addition to our number. Do you think you can unlearn speech? To communicate only at need, and by using the

16

hands?" She made a flowing gesture that held meaning, though he could not quite read it.

Lehnik felt words rise to his lips, but he forced them back and drove them inside his mind. Instead of speaking, he made the sign of assent that his guide had made to him. Here he might rest from slaughter, for a time.

He might live to see Cylla grow up, perhaps even to become such a girl as the one in the water, who had defeated her attackers in the corridor. He might find friendships that were not limited to war or wine or sex. Perhaps, at last, he might find one who would share his mature years.

Yet that was a secondary consideration. There was something powerful here. He had felt it in that garden; it sang along the silent corridors and in the room where he stood. It had filled that over-warm chamber where the Keeper of the Children held sway. It was a cold, clean thing that refreshed his weary spirit.

He gazed at the Sister, who stood silent, a pillar of white topped with an ebony face, and she smiled into his eyes.

"Welcome home, Lehnik," she said.

CHAPTER TWO

The Sister regarded him seriously, her black eyes filled with compassion. "It is no easy task that you will undertake," she said to Lehnik. "Indeed, there is no more difficult apprenticeship existing in the world we know.

"Here you will learn to control the beast that is only a vehicle for the mind. You must do it for yourself, as all of us have done, without guidance or help, for each individual must find his way, and every way is different. There are no rules to learn, no set pattern of behavior that will make the work less onerous."

Lehnik quirked an eyebrow. For all his life he had been patterned to verbal instructions and commands. Communication meant *words*, and it left a blank space in his mind when he thought of having no words to guide him in this new life. Yet he managed to hold in his questions. He did not speak but listened as the Speaker went on.

She smiled at his obvious bewilderment. "Yes, it is difficult. To some it is impossible, but we do not think less highly of those. If they choose they may go down the mountain to work among the lay Sisters. Many do that, in fact." She surveyed him closely.

"I think you will be one who will find the Life compatible, Lehnik. There is a look to you that speaks of someone bedeviled by too many words in his life and too little time for patient thought. I can see in your eyes the trapped thoughts that have been suppressed and frustrated for lack of opportunity to be examined and assessed. Now we shall see if those can come forward and make themselves felt at last."

The bell-pull she touched was the color of the wall, almost invisible. But another Sister came into the chamber and stood quietly, relaxed and without any of the military bearing Lehnik automatically expected.

The Speaker looked at him thoughtfully. "First we will give you a view of your own history. There are too few out in the world who think about understanding themselves and fewer still dream that this world is not the planet that produced our kind, originally.

"Our order keeps the record of that heritage, among other matters. For now you will be shown the face of one of those remote ancestors who first arrived here. Later there will be other things, if you become one of us."

She moved to put her white-gloved hand on his shoulder. "We do not explain what you will see. It will explain itself, and you must decide for yourself why we keep these facts locked into the heart of our mountain and out of the hands of those who might make a chaos of Trans-Kell.

"There will be questions raised that will torture you. The secrets we must keep seem, at times, to be inhumanly restrictive. We know that, but we are bound by ancient oaths. For this reason you must know those secrets, and only this rigorous training will help you to keep silent when you feel the need to speak of them."

The other Sister now came forward holding a white robe that had hung against the wall. Until she lifted it down he had not seen it.

Understanding what he must do, Lehnik doffed his fur cape and leather tunic. He wrapped those soft white folds about him, recognizing the touch of fine wool. There was something subtly comforting in its concealment, as he arranged the hood over his head and the veil about his face.

As he turned to follow the second Sister, the Speaker spoke again. "Think of this, Lehnik. It is a fact that never occurs to anyone until it is brought forcibly to their attention.

"Why is it that the people living in Trans-Kell and her neighbors vary so greatly? Some are black, like me. Others are brown-skinned, some yellow, some pinkish white. Every one of the populated nations contains some of every kind of us. It is as if those who came first deliberately settled some of every sort in each location. It is a strange thought, Lehnik, but give it due consideration. If you find a reason why this was done, then let me know. I have always been curious."

He bent his head again and made the sign of assent with his hands. Then the Sister led him out of the room. The door closed behind them with a whisper that held a note of finality.

Again they traveled infinities of corridors and stairs, each white and featureless except for the differing statues on their pedestals. As the two went down, Lehnik began noticing those carved figures more closely. They represented no animal or man that he had ever

19

seen. As he studied them he decided that they represented thoughts, not things.

The notion excited him—where had it come from? Once he entertained it, the notion fascinated him, and he became certain that he was right. These were ideas cut into marble.

One seemed about to take off and fly into the air. Another sat quietly, emitting a feeling of contentment. A third seemed to compel him to some action, though it was unclear what it might be. He had never thought that such emotions could be held by silent stone.

They reached the bottom of the last of the stairs. No downward flight remained before them, but a smooth corridor was lined with niches shadowed into the white walls. The Sister clicked her fingers once, twice. From several of the niches white-swathed figures stepped forth, their curved blades held before them. They seemed to regard Lehnik with interest as he passed, following his guide.

It was strange. As he went between the thin ranks, he felt something batter at the edges of his mind like moths against a lamp glass or wings against the impalpable air. What was it? Something inside him said, "Thought at the edge of perception," but he was not yet prepared to accept that concept.

Now the Sister turned down a side corridor and set her fingers into a set of grooves that ornamented a carven circle. The design looked like a sun, but at her touch the segment of stone into which the carving had been cut turned smoothly and soundlessly on some hidden pivot. That revealed a doorway, and she gestured for him to follow her into the opening.

This was another such passage, he thought, as that leading from the House of the Children. Yet that hall had been warm and damp, and this was chill and dry, with the tang of something alien hanging in the air. It was the scent of oil and metal and something else that he had never smelled before.

Their steps clattered on the floor, echoing through the darkness as if they moved through a great cavern or chamber, but it was too dark to see. His guide held his sleeve in a firm grip, seeming to need no light in order to find her way.

Lehnik almost opened his lips to ask, but he closed them again firmly and bit them to keep them locked together. All his soldier's instinct told him that this place was dangerous, filled with unfamiliar perils. Yet he recalled the Speaker's face, kind and concerned but firm as steel.

20

He must trust his life to these strangers. That was the beginning, he was suddenly certain, of the discipline he must learn. One who could not trust others could not trust himself.

Beside him in the darkness, his guide chuckled, and that was the first sound he had heard from her—him?—since she had entered the Speaker's chamber. He smiled, feeling that he had passed some test, solved some puzzle correctly.

What could it have been? Only his musing on trust came to mind, and that simple matter came into focus. It was a concept totally alien to the world from which he had just come, but something within Lehnik relaxed slightly. His feet clacked against the stone with more confidence. Perhaps this would not be such a difficult undertaking, after all.

Then he realized that he was seeing. The faintest light had entered the place so gradually that he hadn't noticed it until he found himself staring at the shape of his guide. She was slightly ahead of him, and even so near he couldn't quite decide which sex she might be.

Not too tall, yet tall enough, she could be a tall woman or a short man. Not heavily built, from her walk, she gave the feeling of strength with every movement.

He realized something that had nagged at him since he entered this house. Those whom he met had no odor, either masculine or feminine. Out in the world from which he came, few were fastidious about personal cleanliness. Men reeked of sweat and urine and sometimes blood. Women often had an overripe stink that was both arousing and slightly sickening.

Here you could not tell the sex of anyone by sniffing. All he caught from his companion was a whiff of soap.

Even as the impact of her disapproving thought rebuked him, he caught a breath of his own stink. Used as he was to it, suddenly he felt the need to wash himself as quickly as possible.

Now the light grew stronger, revealing an arched opening that was closed by a pair of wooden leaves into which glass was let. The Sister set her hand against the right panel, and the door opened without hesitation. They stood in a low-ceiled chamber that extended to right and left and straight before him. He could not see very far, because the space was divided into rows of items that the warrior could not identify.

The Sister pointed left, and Lehnik turned to follow her as she picked her way along a cluttered path to a spot at which the walls of boxes and other objects curved to form a small room. In its center

21

was a pedestal of white marble, and upon that sat a small box, black as the Speaker's skin, yet without her polished luster.

A motion from his guide sent him to sit on a bench against a wall of boxes. She touched something on the black box, and it hummed faintly for a moment. Then Lehnik almost came upright. Shapes were forming above that box, as the light dimmed around him. The image above the box became clearer.

A mottled sphere, green and white and brown, hung against the darkness behind it. A voice spoke in a tongue that was like his own and yet subtly different. He could understand, if he concentrated, and he strained to catch every word.

"This is Urth, the home world of our kind. Many millennia ago, its inhabitants discovered the techniques that could be used to travel not only between worlds but between suns and even galaxies. They were restless and ambitious people, set upon putting the seal of their presence upon every world that was suitable for our kind of life.

"This sort of planet is hard to find in any area of the known universe, yet our ancestors explored afar and found what they could. Upon those they placed colonies, limited in numbers but supplied with the means by which to grow and prosper until they, too, might travel outward again in search of new conquests."

The picture changed, and a long shape hovered in darkness that was speckled with stars. Colored vapors gusted from its narrow end, giving the illusion of great speed. Behind it dots of brightness began to flow past it, streaking and changing constantly. Again the voice took up its tale.

"In ships like this that held the seeds of life for men, animals, plants, and even birds and fish, our kind went out to settle the worlds they had discovered. Some perished on worlds holding some subtle danger or difference that would not allow our kind to thrive. Others became the ancestors of populations on teeming worlds filled with the things Mankind values."

The picture shifted again. Another spherical shape formed, this one mostly blue, with one broken green-brown continent showing beneath its tracks of cloud. The picture enlarged, as if Lehnik were drawing nearer and nearer as the voice spoke again.

"This is Halash, our world. The crew of the ship woke our distant ancestors from their frozen sleep and transferred them to the largest land mass on this watery world. With them they sent mechanisms that could create most things needed to nurture the embryos of beasts and plants and people. The things necessary to keep Urth-born people in health would be grown here.

"But in growing those things, many of the natural systems of this world were displaced and destroyed, for preserving them was not the goal of the colonists. Survival and procreation were their first priorities. In the first millennium, they spread over this continent and all the larger islands, and even as I speak they are once more beginning the old cycle of overcrowding and war."

The picture shifted yet again. A battlefield sprang into focus, so realistically that Lehnik could almost smell the blood, though he knew those pictured must have been dead for generations. The familiar cut and thrust of hand to hand combat, the rains of arrows and volleys of thrown spears made him shiver. He had learned to hate the battlefield and he disliked being reminded of that part of his life.

"For this reason, our order has withheld from leaders and populations alike a number of secrets for which we are responsible. Left with our ancestors were weapons that make killing both easy and impersonal. There are techniques that delay death in the old and that preserve life in those who are weak or defective. Such things, we know from our records, drove our distant kin on Urth to excesses and atrocities.

"Our kind has suffered enough. We cannot in good conscience contribute, once more, to the agony of our kind on this clean world. There has been enough, and we would like for it to end here."

Now a face hung above the black box, its gaze fixed on Lehnik. He looked into the face of a man who must be now long dead, the skin yellowish, the eyes myopic. It was not beautiful, but it was somehow likeable, and it spoke directly to him.

"We have preserved the weapons, the techniques, the knowledge left in our care, though we know we will not pursue further expansion, as our ancestors intended for us to do. Spreading in ever-widening circles of destruction is not the ambition of the wise.

"New worlds do not make new people. We have learned to our sorrow that each time our kind ruins a world it simply moves on to find another to ruin. This does not contribute to the well-being of our species nor does it force us to develop wiser ways. On this one world, with this single population of diverse races, we will stop until we have become mature enough to trust ourselves."

The eyes were infinitely sad, and the mouth drooped at the corners as the voice continued, "For this to occur, there must be trustworthy teachers and leaders who will be worthy examples for those they teach and lead. You who watch this hologram are a candidate for such a role. Think of what I have said and upon the experiences of your own life that have led you to this place.

23

"You may become a person who can help to further the growth of our species on Halash. I hope that you will. Good fortune to you."

The face blanked out, and the box stopped humming.

The lights rose to their former level, and the Sister motioned for him to stand. Lehnik came to his feet, feeling as if he had just waked from a spell. His mind boiled with questions, speculations, and excitement.

His lips opened, and he turned eagerly toward the Sister. Her expression warned him, though she made no motion to stop him. He caught himself, closed his lips, and bit them until he could taste blood.

Think. He must think, long and hard, about what he had just heard, as well as about many other things. That had to be the first step in this new life.

Again the Sister chuckled.

Encouraged, Lehnik smiled at her as she turned to the doorway. He followed her from the room and back down the dark corridor, but he was thinking about other things. Automatically, he retraced his steps, and this time the Sister did not have to lead him by the sleeve.

CHAPTER THREE

Lehnik lay in his cubicle, staring into the night. About him in the dormitory lay dozens of other candidates for the Sisterhood, each lying on a cot with a firm pad and covered by a thin layer of wool. Each of them must, he thought, have shivered through many a long night before finding it within himself to ignore the chill by an act of will.

He sighed and turned, his warrior's ears tuned to catch any sound. That was a habit that he felt he would do best to keep.

He heard nothing. For seven nights he had gone to bed in his compartment, and not once had he heard a whisper or a mutter from a sleeper. Not even snores broke the silence. Those who rested here were learning to control every aspect of their lives, and sleep was no exception.

Lehnik had spent more than half his three decades of life sleeping among other men's grunts and moans and snorts. In barracks, encampments, field outposts he had experienced such communal sleep arrangements. Aside from idle talk, perhaps sudden quarrels or blows, there had been the simple noises of sleeping human beings.

He had often waked to sudden cries in the night, sometimes from his own lips, for soldiers often relived dangers and deaths. He was used to having his rest broken by such outcries.

Here, except for the whisper of cloth on cloth from time to time, there was no such living sound. That told him a great deal about the quality of those who slept beside him.

Though the Speaker had urged thought, he had found that by day there was little time for deep thinking. Arms drills, excursions up and down the surrounding mountains using every technique that generations of mountaineers had invented for conquering the heights, treks across seemingly impassable terrain had occupied the past week.

Only when he lay down at night did Lehnik find the opportunity to think about the variety of incomprehensible matters with which he came into contact every day. It cut into his sleep, but he could feel something inside him expanding as he worked at his nightly ruminations.

By day he worked with a squad of twenty Sisters. He had no more idea now than at the beginning which of them might be male and which female. Some gloved hands were smaller than others. Some figures were shorter. Yet he knew those were not dependable indications.

Every member of the squad exerted total effort as they went about their training. Lehnik recognized this course of activities as such, for it was very much like that a soldier received, though far more demanding.

He could tell that some of his companions had prior training, for they handled their weapons with ease and were skilled at moving as a team. Others were clumsy at the beginning, but even they sharpened their abilities with astonishing quickness.

Experienced at training raw recruits, Lehnik found himself reflecting upon the difference that personal desire could make when it came to learning. These candidates wanted to be where they were and to do what they were learning to do. They were not laggard conscripts, dragooned into an unwanted role, and the difference was startling.

He turned on his cot, as quietly as he could manage. No physical discomfort was keeping him awake. The questions nagged at him for hours every night, and he felt he must sort out all the new information he had been given.

The origin of his kind was one matter he had pushed to the back of his mind. It was a conundrum so huge and frightening that he found he wasn't able to cope with it amid the other stresses he was dealing with every day. The question that puzzled him most was the nature of his species.

He had thought he understood every aspect of mankind. After years in the military life, seeing all kinds of men in dangerous and boring and desperate situations, it seemed logical, but he found he was wrong.

That was what troubled him tonight, moving his body restlessly beneath the woolen blanket. First of all, he and all the men he had known had always had one core of pride, no matter how lacking they might be in other areas. Simply because they were male, they knew themselves to be innately superior.

In Trans-Kell there was no legal advantage, no outward show, but that inner arrogance assured his sex that they were men, and nothing that women might do could diminish it. Though women, in this time of danger, principally operated the businesses and farms and other necessary matters of their country, that conviction remained a reassuring factor in every male he knew.

Yet in this place, among these anonymous people, he found himself accepted as a woman and a Sister. He thought back over all the white-garbed Sisters he had met over the years. Not one had ever flinched at being called Sister by any soldier or trader or farmer. He knew now, however, that some, at least, had been men whose very selfhood should have cringed at being taken for females.

Lehnik smiled into the darkness. He realized that, day by day, he was learning: being human was the important thing. Sex had no relevancy here, and he saw no sign of any of its manifestations among his fellows. He felt no urges in that direction himself, though neither did he feel impotent.

Never before had he felt so energetic, so ambitious. He felt secure and peaceful, as well, though eager for anything that might come next. The spectrum of his sensations should have sent him into turmoil, but instead it had coalesced into a healing calm.

Was this one of the steps in the process the Speaker had mentioned? It was certainly one that he had achieved without help or advice. At first it had sounded difficult and somewhat frightening, as he stood in her white chamber. Now he knew it to be stimulating, beyond anything he had ever known.

The normal burst of desperate energy when going into battle was nothing compared to what he felt now. This was a kind of battle that was far more important than a border skirmish or dealing with a bandit raid. If he could win this one, what might he do in the future?

He closed his eyes, seeing dark circles of red and brown behind his eyelids. His body relaxed, and he no longer felt any of the chill in the dormitory. His limbs were warm and quiet and the goose pimples that had plagued him earlier in his training had disappeared.

He was, he thought, beginning to slip into the mold his order demanded of its candidates.

Some instinct made him fold up his legs, his toes set inside the curves of opposite bent knees, one leg crossed beneath the other. He set his arms above his head, elbows out, forearms forming a straight line against the top of his skull. Now he was two triangles, joined at their apices, their points blunted at his waist.

Stillness circulated through him. That strange posture seemed to generate both repose and alertness. The weariness of the day flowed out of him, leaving him invigorated but resting.

He wondered if any of those beyond the curtain of his cubicle had learned this position. Was this something that came naturally once a person left himself open to his disciplined instincts? What more and better things would he find, as time went forward, within his own spirit?

The thought excited him, and he allowed himself to flow with the energies that moved through him. Why had he always thought that discipline was imposed upon people by other people? It did not have to come from outside or by force, he saw now.

How pitiful that method was. As if a window had opened in his mind, he saw with blazing clarity: such techniques were false and useless, fear disguised as obedience, weak and unbecoming. They injured both the disciplined and the one imposing such sham discipline.

There were other things he had thought were hard-and-fast facts about human beings. Were they, too, delusions fostered by those intent upon controlling their fellows?

He had seen greed among most of the men and women he had observed through his lifetime. He had thought it an inherent and necessary part of the human character, yet here no one owned anything except his own body and his own mind.

No one lacked anything necessary for maintaining life and health, and not one of his fellows seemed to desire anything more than that. At least, in no material sense did they seem to have such desires. This was something he accepted without question.

But how did he know it?

This question darted through his mind with the impact of an arrow. Never had he spoken to or been addressed by any of his fellow trainees. Not one had so much as signaled to him anything other than matters necessary to the project in hand.

How could he be so certain they found the same satisfaction that he was finding in this rigorous training? He was entirely convinced they needed their former lives no more than he did. This was Life. That had been endurance and existence.

More of the Speaker's words came back to him. For some it was impossible, she had said, but the Sisters did not condemn them for that. Instead, they were given the choice of going down the mountain to live among those who had been Sisters and now carried forward the business of maintaining the lives of the order.

Of those beginning the training with him, he could think of no one who was missing from the squad. By now he was sure that any who found the training unbearable or impossible must have realized it and withdrawn.

He had learned one tremendous truth. Greed was not necessarily a part of the condition of *every* human being. Some found equal satisfaction in other things.

Anger and gluttony and lust were probably subject to the same qualification, he decided. When mind and body were tried to the utmost by determined people, there was no time for such trivial matters.

He searched in the place within himself where his own sins had lain, and he found in that vacant space a bud of something else. As a soldier he had equated love with lust, as his fellows had done. Now, as he thought of his featureless, almost bodiless companions, he knew that now something had grown in his spirit that could only be called love.

Lust had always made him uncomfortable, making him feel out of control. It was well lost. This was something based on respect and dependence for survival in hard and dangerous places and projects. It was fed by no physical need and it was fueled by complete trust.

It was fed, he decided as he lay in warm content, by nonphysical things. What of that moment in the hallway, when he had been under attack before being frozen? He had almost heard, within his mind, the thoughts of those who tried his skill against their own. Did the Sisters—or some of them—possess some esoteric ability to speak from mind to mind?

At this point, before this night, he had pushed this notion aside. It set up a troubling resonance, being totally against his conditioning. Now he examined the notion.

He had been told that in battle the Sisters moved with impossible teamwork, meshing skills and tactics, even when they were separated by distances that precluded any signals.

His old master-at-arms never tired of marveling at their abilities. "I was wounded in the first attack," he had said. "I was lyin' behind a bush, hopin' that my own people wouldn't step on me and that the enemy wouldn't have time to see that I was still alive.

"There were four Sisters who'd been sent to our command by the Council, bringin' some message to the Colonel. They'd been caught with us by a sortie from beyond Kell. "I was assigned, look you, to guide the four back to the track they had come on. Not that they needed guidin', make no mistake, but it was a courtesy, like.

"Besides, we'd laid traps and pitfalls for our enemies, and I knew where they were placed. I was to make sure they didn't fall into any of those, as well. But we were separated when the rush came, and somehow they knew I was hurt, away out there where they couldn't see me at all. Two came for me, through the thick of the fightin'."

Lehnik could still see the seamed face, the squinted eyes of the old sergeant as he spoke. "I could see their white robes flashin' in the sunlight as they moved. One was tall and thin, the other short and stocky. A clutch of the enemy would see 'em and be after 'em as fast as a bunch of arrows, but the other would see and trim them away with such ease it was hard to believe."

He'd sighed with admiration. "She made it seem like cuttin' butter. And not one got behind her or caught her unaware. After a bit I was sure they were sendin' signals, somehow.

"That pair pulled me out of a swarm of raiders. The tall one took me on her back while the little one mowed us a path through those hornet-mad fightin' men as if he she might be mowin' daisies in a hayfield. I never saw anybody dodge and dart and handle a blade like that in all my life, and me a master-at-arms!

"They got me over to the other pair, and I guided 'em through our traps and pitfalls. They had dispatches that had to go fast, and I knew by then that nothin' could be faster than them, be they women or demons."

Lehnik had trusted the sergeant's honesty, but he had thought at the time that he might be remembering something that was strongly tinged with gratitude. Now he regarded the tale in a new light. The tall Sister had been a man, he was certain, better able to carry the chunky master-at-arms. The smaller had been typical of the swordsmen of her order, more disciplined and fearless than any among the soldiery.

Now he felt in his heart that they did communicate without speech, and he suspected those Sisters had intuited the dilemma in which the sergeant had found himself. Having come so far, he found himself unwilling to pursue that line of thought further. He didn't care to fantasize about the new picture of the world forming in his mind until he could prove what he hypothesized.

Then he thought of something else the Speaker had said about words. She had mentioned being bedeviled by words, he recalled, and that was another thing that seemed to plague the world below this mountain.

Before he climbed to the House of Silent Women his life had been formed and patterned by words. Words set his limits, aimed his actions, altered his perceptions and his activities. Spoken by those known or unknown, words had shaped his entire existence. Never in all that time had he examined those words for hidden meanings. He had never considered questioning their omnipotence. He had not been allowed the opportunity to do that, he realized.

Now everything was different. Lying in the dark silence of that quiet house, he felt relaxed and self-controlled as never before. Now he could question anything at all and come to his own conclusions.

Lehnik thought, now, about words. Below in the world he knew it had seemed that once men named an object or an idea they had captured its essence. Naming, in some way, was like owning the essential being of the named thing. Now, thinking about the matter, he knew that to name is not the same thing as to define.

But that thought didn't go far enough. To define is not to capture the innate reality. He considered pain as an example...a very good example of his concept.

Let a pedagogue take pain as his subject and write and read volumes on the subject. Let him speak with those who know pain and tell of what he has learned, but still he has no real conception of what it truly is. Not until a tooth goes bad or a leg is broken or his back is wrenched out of plumb will this expert on the subject of pain understand what it is he was trying to describe.

So he had proven to his satisfaction that a word was a dim shadow of the thing it tried to convey and to capture. A word had limited usefulness, and one who spoke the words that sent his fellow men into danger and death also, perhaps, had even more limited usefulness.

Wide-eyed in the night, Lehnik lay thinking of things that had never before come into focus in his mind. Something was growing inside him, moment by moment, thought by thought.

He felt his ability to question expanding painfully, stretching his soldier's training that taught him to obey unquestioningly whatever word was spoken in command. Now the part of him that contained the habit was twisted and rent, torn open so the light of reason could illuminate it.

"Even the Council...." His lips formed the words, but not even a whisper could be heard. "Even the Council itself is not beyond question by anyone, soldier or citizen."

He waited tensely for some power to smite him for that blasphemous thought. About him all was quiet, dark, peaceful.

He thought something even more terrible. *Even officers are not beyond question, or priests, or anyone at all, no matter how important or powerful. Even the Speaker is not beyond question!*

31

Shock raced through him. If he had managed to survive a thousand battles and to live more decades than one might have a right to expect in the soldiering trade, he would never have arrived at a point at which he could think such a thought.

His old life led down a road that went elsewhere, and it held no room for questions. It held only empty words that might well lead to its own extinction.

In the distance, he heard the shriek of a high-ranging veer-hawk. Dawn, he knew, was tinting the edge of the sky and touching the mountain-tops. He had thought and thought until the night was worn away, but he was not at all weary.

He felt alive in every nerve. He seemed to throb with expectancy, and he waited with impatience for all the questions this new day might bring.

CHAPTER FOUR

The training progressed, wordless, demanding constant alertness and decision making on the part of every member of the squad. Unhesitating teamwork, without shouted commands, became second nature to the former soldier.

A time came when Lehnik felt he knew from personal exploration every crag and crevice of the mountain chain holding the peak on which stood the House of his order. He had climbed rock faces that seemed to have no foothold even for a lizard. He had swung a thousand bow-lengths over gorges, held by a pair of hands that seemed entirely too small to trust with his life. He had trusted, and he was alive.

Now his squad was a cohesive unit. They had worked out signals using hand movements and finger-clicks, without any word to expand on them. Whistles bridged the distances across which motions of the hands could not be seen clearly. Snaps of the fingers now spoke to him as clearly as any shouted order had ever done in his military career.

Once they were masters of the mountains, they spent weeks more in the forests cloaking the sides and feet of the heights. Lehnik had believed ambush to be one skill he had completely conquered and understood thoroughly. Once he began training with the Sisters, he found they could move through the thickest undergrowth without stirring a twig or sending a bird shooting from its perch. He learned from them to scoop up messengers or troops in nets that were invisible to those who walked over their meshes, which were cunningly concealed by ferns and mosses.

He developed a sixth sense that warned of deathtraps, some of which dropped invaders into pits and skewered them on sharpened stakes. He learned about all the kinds of live-traps that procured prisoners for questioning.

Lehnik did not question the need for these bloody skills. His life and the history of Trans-Kell had taught him the necessity for such matters, for invasions crossed the Kell and the other borders as regularly as the phases of the three moons occurred in the sky. Raids came weekly in the lowlands.

The ancient man who had left the holographic message had understood his species to a nicety. Peaceful pursuits were not yet a part of the human race.

Now questions poured through Lehnik's mind, intoxicating him with unlimited possibilities. Was this single House the caretaker of all of those weapons and devices of which the man had spoken? Were all the artifacts of the star-farers stored somewhere beneath the massive structure that crowned the crag?

It seemed unreasonable that it would be so, for Halash was now well populated, with orders of Sisters in every nation. Surely they, too, would care-take the secrets left by those first colonists. It might be that each group guarded a different array of such equipment and techniques. That would make sense, he thought.

Each country's Sisterhood, with its strong House that he now knew to be filled with unspoken thoughts and hidden treasures, was the hidden heart of the nation. Not only Trans-Kell, he was certain, drew its rulers from those trained by the Order. Other nations, he knew well, used the Sisterhood's services as incorruptible repositories of important documents and carriers of vital messages.

His own House was still unknown to Lehnik, for his training had taken him with his squad, ranging over the countryside through blizzards and thaws and the first weeks of spring. Now he found himself wondering what else the place might hold and what might be the work of those who had done with their training.

There came a day when he learned more. His group had completed the first round of their training and the Sister who was their leader indicated there was time for rest. She showed them lighter robes, suitable for wear inside the warm building, and she showed them where to stow their weapons and ropes and other tools.

Turning to a stair of golden stone, which seemed bathed in sunlight, she led them upward. It led into a corridor of the same warm marble, which was guarded from regularly spaced niches by statues carven from every shade of natural rock. Rosy spirals marked one, and Lehnik felt that to be a happy color. Another rounded shape was the deep blood-brown tint of a planet, filled with patient strength.

He slowed his steps so as to look at the carvings more closely. The Sister clicked her fingers, not impatiently but firmly, and he hurried after her, still wanting to see those fascinating shapes at his leisure.

At the end of the corridor was a door whose surface was painted the blue of a summer sky. When the Sister touched it, the panel swung open to reveal a room that blazed with varicolored light raying from lamps made of jewel-hued glass. In its center there was a polished oval of wood, many bow-lengths in circumference, with cushions spaced about it, along with chairs and stools. All were painted the shade of garnets.

The seats were occupied by Sisters, but Lehnik had to look twice before he was certain these brightly robed figures were actually those of the Sisters he knew only as robed in white. But he recognized one by her gesture of welcome, another by her walk as she came to greet the newcomers.

Hands moved in the graceful sign language.

Come!

Welcome!

Sit here!

The meanings were as clear as any words could have made them. He moved into the circle and sat on a cushion beside a stool where a rose-clad Sister was sitting. One of her hands touched him lightly on the shoulder to get his attention. Then she pointed toward the end of the chamber, where gold-shot curtains were parting.

A tall figure came through them and let them swing shut behind her. She took her place in the center of the circle and waited.

Again the hand tapped Lehnik's shoulder, and he turned to see a group of veiled musicians enter and take up the instruments that had been lying among the cushions. It had been a very long time since he had heard real music. The songs of soldiers or the ditties heard in taverns were no substitute for the harmonies he had learned as a child in the home of his parents.

The long stem of the *octor* sighed a contralto note. The stringed *ruballes* were bowed, plucked, and strummed by expert hands, forming contrapuntal melodies. How he had missed music!

Motion caught his eye, and he turned his head to see the tall shape in the circle begin to dance. Its robes of palest green moved on the air like the wings of gossamer flies. The dancer's leg extended, curved high, as her arms floated on the music-laden air. She tensed, stretched, and whirled, her robe swirling around her lithe body.

Lehnik felt dizzy as the music purled about him and the dancer floated on the rhythms like a swan upon water. He was no stranger

35

to the arts, for his father and mother had, before their deaths, been prosperous merchants who supported dancers and musicians, painters and sculptors with both money and their presence.

They had advised the Council on artistic matters, for it was widely known their taste was impeccable. Before a raid into the outskirts of the city had demolished their home and killed both of them, they had given their son and their daughters rounded educations in both the arts and the sciences. All that conditioning awoke inside Lehnik now, as he watched and listened and remembered.

Now the dancer spun to a halt, one arm pointing upward while green veils settled quietly to rest about her. Lehnik touched his hands together and bowed his head in the signal of highest praise.

As she sank onto a cushion, the rose-robed Sister beside the former soldier rose and stepped onto the smooth wooden floor. Now the musicians throbbed a rhythm so infectious that he found himself swaying in time, while the rosy shape stepped and swayed, moved hands and toes and head in comical motions. Her audience began to laugh, and Lehnik found himself smiling behind his veil.

When his neighbor finished her dance she turned and caught his hand, trying to pull him to his feet in turn. But he shook his head, raised one hand and twined two fingers together. Then he indicated a tangle-footed fall, and there was another laugh.

Now a scarlet dancer rose to take her turn. Returning to his seat, Lehnik felt for the first time that there was no shame in his failure to find an art that compelled him and at which he excelled. As he had grown up the lack of a talent had troubled him, but now that old ache subsided.

As he watched her bright shape spin, he realized there were no quarrels or disagreements in this place. Where no words were spoken, there could be no argument. For the first time he understood what a wonderful thing that could be in a world plagued by squabbling.

Varied and fascinating as the dancing was, he tired of watching it at last. He had seen several of the white-clad Sisters leave the room beside one of the bright-robed ones, and he thought there might be another place and another art he might explore.

As if she heard his thought, the Sister who had brought him here came to his side and motioned toward the doorway through which the other group had gone. Lehnik rose to follow her, and she led him into the hall where sculptors worked.

So she had noticed his interest in the works along the corridor, he thought. And she cared enough to take him to see where the pieces had been made.

This was a place where he might have spent hours or even days. Those who worked there were garbed in rough gray stuff that showed stone dust only minimally. Their hands were calloused and strong, and their chisels moved through granite or marble with accurate strokes, seeming to work the stone so easily that Lehnik marveled. Wonderful things grew beneath the sculptors' magical fingers.

The Sister indicated a vacant stool before the long bench that was the work table. There was a pedestal there, holding a lump of clay. Intrigued, Lehnik sat and thrust his fingers into the cool mass, feeling it give beneath his movements. Could this be the art that he had craved all his life?

But his fingers were awkward, feeling no oneness with the clay. No matter how he prodded and pummeled the stuff, there was no pulse of life in it that told him what it should become. He stood and shook his head.

The tall Sister stared at him piercingly and set her finger against her veil at the jaw line as if thinking hard. Then with a decisive nod she turned and beckoned him from the room and down the bright corridor. Away they went along the intricate route that had brought him, that first time, from the House of Children.

Lehnik thought of Cylla, and he felt a throb of excitement. He would like to see her again, even to watch her grow and to help her learn. He sighed, thinking how unlikely that was.

Now they were in the corridor he had entered so many weeks before. A bell hanging from the cornice received a brisk spin from the Sister, and its tiny tingle brought the Matron from her room at once.

"Ah, now, have we one here who wants to work with the young ones?" she asked in her busy manner. "Seldom do we find that, nowadays, though when I was much younger many sought to work with the children. Too few come, these days, to help Bertha with her tasks. Come along, then. We'll see how you fare with the small ones."

Before he could make any sign, she bustled him through the curtained door into a rather plain room fitted with a desk, two chairs, and a couch long enough for sleeping on. Lehnik turned to wave to the Sister who had brought him there, but she was already going back along the corridor toward the passage leading to the House.

Bertha was already at her endless stream of talk. "Now you must understand that the children must be talked to. I know how you in the Order value your silence, and I can respect it, if I cannot *understand* it. But youngsters must know the language of their country, and know it from intelligent and well spoken people.

"They need to learn how to think in words, as everyone must know how to do, whether Sister or soldier or child. That is why the children are separated from the Order. We teach them, as well, history and mathematics and sciences of both life and matter. We show them how to write a fair hand and we do stress correct spelling!" She stared at him sharply, and he nodded, though he had never had more than moderate success at spelling.

He found his tongue had grown stiff with disuse, and the words were rusty in his mouth. "I understand," he said, "but I am not certain I am suited to this. Might I try it for a time and see how the children like me and how well I do at teaching them?"

She said, "Of course. 'Tis the only way. Some are not suited to deal with the young rapscallions, for patience is the most important matter you need. After that you will need the answers to every question known to man, woman, or child, and more, too.

"No, Sister, it's always this way. You try yourself against the task, and if you feel suited to it you stay. Otherwise you go back to your precious silent Life, with my blessing."

That relieved his mind enough to allow him to ask the question uppermost in his heart. "I brought a child here, some months back. Her name is Cylla, and she is about three, very fair and quiet. Do you know her?"

Bertha smiled broadly. "Indeed I do. I know them all. She's a good child, already well on her way to knowing her own mind. She has not been made difficult by that, either, for she's a sensible little thing. You would like to see her." It was not a question.

"I would. Very much," Lehnik said.

"Then come with me to the mathematics class. She's there, I'll warrant, for she took to her *abbak* like a bird to the air. She's a fair wonder with numbers and calculations, though they are nothing but a mystery to me."

They pattered down another hall, set at an angle to the first, to a room that was very wide and quite long. It was divided into spaces where groups of children worked with paper and pen or with bead-strung instruments, and he recognized the *abbak* with fondness.

That ancient instrument for calculating went back much farther than human history on Halash, he now understood. Dozens of the devices lay on the long tables or were clacking busily in small hands.

One was being used by Cylla herself, her small fingers whipping the beads along the wires while her lips moved silently, expressing the problem she was working with. It was amazing that one so young had grasped the principles so well, he thought as he watched.

As if feeling his glance, she raised her fair head and saw him. Her blue eyes rounded with pleasure, although, swathed as he was in the robes of a Sister, he hadn't expected she could recognize him.

With the sure instinct of the very young, Cylla rose and flew into his arms. "Lehnik! You came back!" she cried.

He caught her up and hugged her close, feeling again the special warmth between them. "Indeed, I never left you. I became a Sister and moved next door, where I have been all this long while. I have been learning all the things a Sister must know, which is why I have not returned to see you."

He held her away and looked into her small face. "How have you been, Cylla? Are you happy here?"

She surveyed his veiled face solemnly. Then a giggle shook her. "Krohm would be mad, if he knew," she whispered into his ear.

Lehnik laughed again. He never had suspected that the mite the officer Krohm had handed to him after that last engagement had understood any of what went on about her. Now he thought she had known precisely what had taken place. He hugged her again.

"But are you happy?" he asked again.

"Oh yes. Bertha and the Sisters are kind, and they know so very much. We learn all sorts of things in the school. And then we clean and cook—or at least I'm learning to—and we work with leather and wood and stone. Making things, you know."

She smiled even more widely as she said, "And in spring we will grow things in the garden. Bertha says we will grow our own flowers and herbs and vegetables and we'll dry and preserve everything we can. It will be fun."

Lehnik set her down and took her small hand. "I would like to meet the other children. How many are there?"

"Twenty," she said. "Bertha says usually there are even more, but the raids have...killed so many." Her blue eyes filled with tears, and he remembered her mother's death. Had she seen?

To divert her mind, he asked, "I thought the war would have brought more, rather than fewer."

Behind him, Bertha said, "For every one it brings like Cylla, there are more who go down to the lowlands to visit their kin and never come back because of the raiders."

He squeezed the child's hand, recalling the scene at the farmstead where his troop had found her. There had been dead children there, the offspring of farm laborers, he remembered.

But she tugged him by the hand to a group of the smaller children. Toddlers held up their arms to him, and three- and four-year-olds plied him with questions, while Cylla stood back and watched, her attitude strangely proprietary.

Lehnik sat down among the smallest. "I am going to help care for you and teach you," he said. "Come close, and we will get to know each other."

They scrambled for the limited space in his lap, and the honor went to a pair of toddlers, boys with sandy hair and dark eyes, as alike as twins ever could be. As everyone settled into place, Lehnik felt his free hand caught in a warm grasp.

Cylla was there too, a look of contentment on her elfin face.

CHAPTER FIVE

Lehnik found his time in the Children's House one of the strangest of his life, since the deaths of his parents. He was assigned, with seven other sisters and Bertha, to care for the twenty children, to teach them, and to train them in skills he had never thought of conveying to anyone so young.

They were taught the basics of self protection, both hand-to-hand combat and swordsmanship. They were exercised to build muscle and wind, after which they took up archery, rock-climbing, and tracking through the frozen heights or the forested slopes. When spring freed them from winter's hold, they fled the confines of the Children's House for the freedom of the outdoors.

Cylla was too young, as yet, to take the warrior training Lehnik found was to be his principal responsibility. Five children were assigned to him. Geste and Bella were twins, tall and dark-haired, as alike as brother and sister could possibly be. Rollin was freckled and fair, afraid of nothing to an extent that terrified Lehnik.

Pasca was shy and pale as a spring flower, only six years old. She seemed too vulnerable to risk at such dangerous practice, but he found her tough and determined. Eliva, the twelve-year-old, took her in charge, as she did everyone, including Lehnik himself. Self-possessed and assuming responsibility for things far beyond her years, she was, he thought, a Sister-to-be. She had all the prerequisites, including alarming self control.

This lively crew, it turned out, taught him as much as he could teach them. They learned woodcraft with speed and enthusiasm, and after only a few weeks they contrived and carried out against him an ambush that took him totally by surprise.

They soon learned to scamper along the rock faces like so many cliff-sheep, and often he found the breath catching in his throat as they moved up impossible scarps or rappelled down underslung walls of stone. It was only with much difficulty that he had persuaded them to accept the inconvenience of being roped together, which was the only reason he hadn't lost any of his charges.

They had all the abandon of bodiless spirits until Pasca fell. That sobered them, for if the rope had not been in place, properly anchored by the topmost climber, she would have been lamed or even killed. After that, it was much easier to link his young climbers, and they conquered every height suitable for their ages and experience.

In its way, their work in the schoolroom was as demanding as the field work. Lehnik, years away from his own schooling, found himself taking up works on mathematics, languages (there were many dialects spoken on Halash, the heritage of the divergent races who formed the original colony).

Biology and chemistry were lost in the tangle of his past, and he had to bone up on those, as well, for no child was considered too young to learn at least the rudiments of the great disciplines. His intellect, neglected during his years of soldiering, was honed again to broaden its range and to work at full capacity.

He had rather dreaded having to take part in formal schooling, for he remembered his own with no fondness whatsoever. To his delight, he found the school the Sisters conducted did not resemble that rigid institution at all. It was geared to individual aptitudes, and though discipline was inherent and unstated, it offered freedom to the young minds in its classes.

For specified spans of time, each child was assigned a single field of study and with that he or she continued until the limits of current capabilities were reached. One studied math, one history, one the roots and rhetoric of languages, another the physical sciences. With every learning aid known to their people, the youngsters delved deeply into their specialties, uninterrupted by distractions.

The instructors were there, if needed, but as much as possible they allowed the children to pose their own questions and find their own solutions. While all was not total harmony, the level of the squabbles among the small scholars was on a much higher plane than Lehnik remembered from his own school days.

The youngsters did not misbehave, though their energy levels were high and there was noise and bustle in any room of the school where more than two were assembled. Discipline was quick and just, in the event of disagreements or quarrels.

Lehnik watched with fascinated attention the subtle guidance of these children, who were nudged almost invisibly toward self direction. He knew they would never make ordinary soldiers, ready to obey the most stupid order, though their skill with weapons was already awesome. But not one of his students would ever accept an irrational order or believe an illogical premise.

As each reached mastery of one subject, he or she was put into another. By the time a child reached twelve or so, which seemed to be the upper limit in age at the Sisters' school, he had a sound basic education, which would have been the envy of anyone Lehnik knew who had been prepared to attend the University at Chelos.

Cylla, though in the younger group of children, managed to find the time to see him often. Though he sometimes examined his conscience to find a trace of overindulgence, he continually found her to be more mature, brighter, and more observant than the others in her age group. There was something about her; from the moment Krohm had put her into his arms, weeping bitterly but not hysterical, his heart had gone out to her. Even busy as he was, he managed to keep an eye on her progress and was always pleased at what he found.

Life was now very demanding, though in a far different way from the demands of his earlier training. Every day held much of interest, ranging from important questions to hilarious situations. Not the least of his satisfactions lay in discussing each day's events with the other teachers who shared this odd offshoot of the Order's life.

One evening he was sitting in the common room with the stocky Sister who taught archery and biology. Their hands were busy, but they took advantage of their new situation to talk about their students, too.

At last, feeling somewhat guilty at speaking of personal matters, Lehnik said, "I wonder if you might tell me something. The Speaker never mentioned when I should take the oath of silence, and I never have done that. I couldn't, of course, ask those who trained me. Have you taken it?"

The veiled head turned and a pair of brown eyes creased at the corners with amusement. "Sister! Has it taken you this long to understand that there is no oath of silence? That is something those below invented to explain our lack of words. They cannot conceive of anyone who will not clutter her life with chatter, given the ability. That is why they sometimes claim we cut off our tongues!" There came a chuckle from beneath the veil.

"You will never take such an oath, for it does not exist. When there is need, you will speak, as you do in the school or when deciding the best course for our students. There are those of our Order who walk among the people of Trans-Kell, unveiled, wearing ordinary clothing, speaking when that is called for. They go about our business in that way because it cannot be accomplished otherwise."

Lehnik sighted along the short shaft of the arrow he was making to measure for a ten-year-old's bow. He felt chagrined, for he should have thought of that himself. He found that he had not gone quite far enough in his thinking and his questioning of old assumptions.

He opened his lips. Then he closed them firmly. He needed to think, not to talk, reexamining every truism he had ever known. He finished the arrow and set into it the steel arrowhead, binding the shaft fast about the shank of the point.

He wondered how much of the philosophy of the Sisters found its way into the minds of these children. They were intuitive, and they noticed everything. Perhaps they would go out from this place as fully rational people.

More and more he was realizing that among those he had known in his life outside the Order, few were rational. Would these younglings make an impact on the overall level of thinking in the ordinary world?

He took up a fresh shaft and ran the shaft-straightener along it, his mind now working at full speed. He thought of the past months, the things he had learned about the past of his species on Halash. He considered his own training and the arts he had seen in that other House. This was a hidden enclave of civilization set upon a barbaric world, he thought.

More than that, it was the nurturer of a life so unlike that of the citizens below the mountain, so lacking in any of the normal values held by them, that it would inevitably seem worthless to any who didn't know it from the inside. But once you had experienced the achievements it evoked from your own being, you no longer held to those outworn values.

Once he had been required to gain iron control over both mind and body, to think clearly and objectively, he was freed from the manipulations of society. Now he was, in the truest sense, a law unto himself, but with a major difference.

Whereas those who were lawless among the normal people broke laws or evaded important rules, these who held the most restrictive of controls over themselves posed no threat to others and offered great benefits to any country into which they might go. That was why the Sisters, in every country, were given free access to every city, crossed borders without let or hindrance.

That was why important negotiations, truces, exchanges of prisoners and vital messages were entrusted to them. Immune to argument, totally lacking any desire for wealth or power, they were as nearly incorruptible as humankind seemed to be able to come.

That had to be the reason why so many of the Council of Trans-Kell were members of the Sisterhood.

As subtly as a moth at a window, something nudged at his mind. Almost in words...it had to come from the Sister at his side. Deaf to thoughts as he was, he detected affirmation and agreement. He was right. That was beyond doubt, now that he had thought over the situation.

He glanced aside sharply, but his companion was serenely fletching another arrow. Her gaze was set on her work, and no crinkle of her veil told him she might be smiling. But he knew with certainty that she had heard his thoughts, which only confirmed what he had felt for a long while. Some of the Sisters communicated without speech.

Lehnik rose and stretched the kinks from his bones. Suddenly restless, he found the confines of the room and even of the huge House of Children to be a prickle at his nerves. He looked down at the Sister, who was checking her arrow before setting it in its slot.

She glanced up at him. "It is time," she said. "Go to the Speaker. I, too, have heard the summons. Until you become more adept at accepting our interior speech, you will need assistance, and perhaps she can provide it. Many are resistant to the idea of speaking from mind to mind."

Lehnik bowed his head in farewell and made his way toward Bertha's classroom. He had to go now, even at the cost of leaving Cylla again. There was something that he needed to do, and a command was laid upon him. It came from outside him and from within, too. He was needed, and that was enough.

He made his farewells as quickly as possible. Then he sought out the hidden doorway, and for some reason he had no trouble with locating it. He hurried down the dark stair and found his way, as surely as a migrating bird or a homing fowl.

The Speaker was waiting for him!

CHAPTER SIX

Lehnik had not walked the halls of the Sisters' House since winter, and the spring had been filled with effort and satisfaction. Now the whiteness of the corridors soothed him and calmed his mind. His nerves settled from their disturbance, whatever had caused it, as he moved through the silent passages.

This time no veiled figure darted from a door or a niche to test his skills. This time he knew that he would have dealt with such a trial with even less effort than before.

All around him, the air seemed to ripple with whispers to which he was deaf. Before going to the House of Children he had understood that he was missing the underlying communication that connected many members of the Order. There was no doubt the Sisters knew of his lack, and he wondered how many of his fellows could not detect the patterns of thought linking their companions. Now he felt those thoughts only as the lightest of moth-wings brushing against his mind.

His legs did not weary as he climbed flights of stairs and moved along white corridors. The long days of training, added to other long days of teaching the children on lesser slopes, had hardened him to more than soldierly endurance.

At last he came to the level where the Speaker kept her rooms, but something told him to climb yet again. The small spiral stair beside her door led to the very top of the House, he was certain, and up it he went. At last it led him to a corridor where an open door let a flood of brilliant light into the already well lit hallway.

He entered a room filled with dazzle, striking through a bubble of glass that domed the chamber. Speaker stood beside a long metal tube, through which she was peering. It was much like an officer's spyglass, but it was longer and, he suspected, far more powerful.

He glanced in the direction toward which it was aimed. There lay a deep notch between neighboring peaks, which allowed a glimpse of the grasslands lying along the eastern edge of the mountain chain.

The Speaker turned, hearing his quiet steps. Now she was robed in tough traveling robes, whose whiteness belied their tough weave. When she stepped forward to greet him, Lehnik saw that her narrow feet were shod in riding boots.

She took his arm and led him to the instrument. "Look through here," she said.

Lehnik set his eye to the circle of glass at the narrow end of the tube. Everything blurred for a moment, but the woman turned a knob at the side of the instrument, and when things came clear he nodded and she withdrew her hand.

Now he could see the plain, distant as it was, very clearly. The low hills on the other side of that narrow stretch were a shadow at the farther edge of the flatlands, and beyond that again thick layers of dark smoke rolled skyward in billows.

He thought, even as he stared, of the villages spaced along the River Kell. There was one billow for each of the towns he knew, and he had recently traveled there with Krohm and his troop. The geography was fresh in his mind.

"Raiders?" he asked, shaping the word with his lips but uttering no sound. All the habits of wordlessness seemed to have descended upon him again, once he left the children.

She shook her head. "Far worse," she said. "Invaders." Her black eyes were filled with brightness that was anger as well as something more disturbing. "A House has been breached, Sister Lehnik. Its secrets have been stolen by those who lack the self-control or the judgment for using them." A shiver traveled along her tall shape.

"The Elector of Garrouche has decided he will rule all of Halash, beginning with his neighbor, Trans-Kell. He is a strong man, but he lacks the wit to use anything so dangerous, and he will destroy far more than he bargains for, if the weapons are left in his hands.

"Yet even he is a bit frightened by the things he found in the storage area beneath the House of Garrouche. He is, as yet, cautious about using them. So his forces, so far, have come, using only common weapons, and only if ordinary means fail will the Elector bring out the devices he found in the care of our Order."

Lehnik straightened from bending to look through the instrument. The question he asked needed no words, being plain in his gaze.

She answered it at once. "We ride today. Now. Riding gear waits in your old cubicle, and your horse that brought you here is saddled. My own and the pack animals are ready. We go to consult the Council at Chelos, and I have chosen you to come with me, for reasons that seem good to me. Get ready and meet me in the stables."

Lehnik lost no time. His military experience had been horrific enough, and the thought of what might be done to the people of his country made him feel sick and angry. The man he had seen in that ancient holograph had hinted at weapons far worse than the worst the colonists had been able to make in the generations since they came to this world.

He thought of the officers he had known. Not one, even Krohm, would have known how to use such weapons, and few had possessed the common sense to understand what damage they might do to friend and foe alike. He might well be at the end of the civilization that had been built so painfully on Halash.

He arrived at the stables quickly, his travel pack in hand, to find Speaker waiting. They rode forth along a path that no one unfamiliar with the terrain might ever have suspected of existing. The tall ferns of spring hid it even from the riders, and the horses seemed to find it with their hooves and their instincts.

Neither Sister spoke. Not only habit dictated their silence, Lehnik knew. He was sure her thoughts, as his did, busied themselves with the task at hand. This visit to the Council must be made as quickly as possible. Even now all Sisters must be being recalled to the defense of their Houses, in every country on the continent.

The battles in Trans-Kell must go forward without the aid of others in the Order who lived outside the borders of that country. When Speaker broke her silence at last, she explained why. "Our House in Garrouche was overwhelmed by great numbers of troops, brought against it without warning. Many of the Sisters were out about the business not only of the Order but of the Elector himself. It was the basest of treacheries, and it succeeded.

"That House was not protected by mountains, as ours is. It was dug into the hills of Garrouche, true, but it can be approached without difficulty, and it is within the City itself. It would have been defensible, if all its complement had been present, but they were not, for the Elector had taken care to send too many on long and difficult missions."

Lehnik asked, "With the Order's ability to communicate from mind to mind, could they not have read his thoughts in order to know what he planned?"

She stared at him as if appalled at the thought. "Without his knowledge and consent? That would be blasphemy. Even the Elector's crime is not as great as that would have been.

"No, honor is our only possession. Integrity is our principal weapon, when all is said. We cannot look into the minds of those who are not Sisters, for we will not. We grant to everyone the right to his own uninvaded thought."

Lehnik nodded slowly, saying nothing. He should have realized that, for it was implicit in everything he had come to understand in his inward journeying as a part of the Order.

They rode side by side across the steep pass and down into the grasslands beyond. The track they now followed was not marked by recent hoof prints of any traveler, single or in company. The droppings of horses were old and dried, some crumbling into the soil and sprouting tiny blue flowers from the richness deposited there.

"There should have been traders coming this way before now," Speaker said. "It is time for replenishing stores, after the long winter. It is obvious those invaders have disrupted the normal life of Trans-Kell, of they would have passed this way, and already the people lower on the mountain would be dickering with them for goods."

They kicked their beasts forward, and after that they rested their mounts only when they knew they must. Before nightfall on the second day of their journey they reached the Inn of the Middle Way.

At that point, the road leading through the mountains intersected another that followed a minor stream northward toward Chelos and the arm of the sea that served Trans-Kell as its major seaport. They stopped at the Inn, for they were weary and their mounts must have rest and grain.

They found the innkeeper to be a frightened man. His small gray eyes lighted with relief when he saw the two Sisters entering his common room. He bustled forward to meet them, all a-chatter with nervous talk, which hid his fears poorly.

"Welcome, Sisters, to the Inn of the Middle Way. Boy, see to their horses! Do you have pack animals? Boy, see to all their animals. Fresh water and plenty of grain, remember!"

As the boy ran out to tend their mounts, he turned to his human guests. "This way, Sisters. My wife has just this moment taken a pot of fresh soup from the fire. It is thick with meat from the mountains

49

and our own spring vegetables. New bread is still hot, as well. You have arrived at a good time." He gestured toward a table, already set with thick dishes and cups.

It was as well that Sisters had no need of speech, for they would have had no chance to speak, even if they had been so disposed. He kept a running chatter as he ordered their food to be brought from the kitchen.

The table was in a quiet corner, though it was obvious the inn was not overwhelmed with business. Two drovers hunched over a table near the front of the room. A single man, who had the look of a horse dealer, lounged on a bench beside the kitchen door.

Speaker made washing motions with her gloved hands. The innkeeper pointed to a door leading out the back of the inn. "We've a pump and a horse trough there, and you can wash all you like," he said. "Clean water from our well, none better, Sisters!"

Lehnik pumped a clear stream into the trough, while Sister unwound her veil and took off her gloves to scrub the dust and sweat of the journey away. In his own turn, he washed and drank from his cupped hands. In that respect the innkeeper told the truth. He had never tasted better water. He had also been accurate about the quality of the food. The strong hot soup and the still spongy bread were wonderfully flavorful and filling. As they ate, drinking thin ale with the food, Lehnik listened to the innkeeper, for the little man seemed anxious to talk.

"Ill tidings have traveled across the hills from the east. Ridding-town is burnt, did you know that? A drover told me, just this morning, though there was little need for anyone to bring the news. From my front door I can see the smoke boiling above the hills." He bustled away to the kitchen in reply to a shrill call, but in a moment he was back.

"Lewesvale's badly damaged, they say, with many of the people driven out and others killed and burning with their houses. All the troops, he says, have been pulled back into the hills, leaving Kell-ford unguarded. They must intend to try to hold the raiders away from the towns farther west. They have to keep them away from Chelos, too." He shuddered.

"If the capital should go, we'd be cut off from the sea. No trade would go forward. Without the seagoing trade connecting this land with the rest along the edge of the continent, things would be bad. Very bad."

Now the man who had lounged on the bench stood and came to stand beside their table. He had a thin, clever face, tracked deeply by wrinkles, though he was not yet old, it was plain from his youthful movements.

He bent and spoke to the Speaker. "Is it permitted that I join you? I have come westward from Kell, and I have seen many things. I take it you are going toward Chelos, and likely you mean to talk—pardon, I mean to meet—with the Council."

With a nod, Speaker gestured for the man to take a stool from an adjoining table and pull it up to theirs. He did so and sat, laying his flat leather hat on the table and looking closely at the pair of them for a moment.

The innkeeper, standing behind him, drew a quick breath. "The Sisters are roused to action by this invasion?" he asked.

Speaker nodded.

"Ah. Then perhaps there is some hope still. I have never seen the Order take a hand in any matter they did not manage to turn to good for the country."

The stranger leaned forward. "There is something I must tell you, and I know that in some manner you will convey my message to the Council without breaking your vows."

Again Speaker nodded.

"I purchase mounts from breeders in the grasslands and sell them from Garrouche to Chelos, west into Horniche on the other side of the mountains, and as far south as Chervalle. Two days ago I was crossing Kell at the ford with a string of horses to sell at the spring fairing at Selni, just across the border in western Garrouche.

"The ford was in flood with the spring rains, so I camped for the night on this side, so as to cross by day." He cocked his head, his narrow gray eyes seeing something within his memory. "Come dawn, three Sisters came riding out of the east and forded the river without taking time to check the depth or the speed of the flood." He looked at the Speaker thoughtfully.

"I have ridden many times in company with Sisters. I have met bandits with them and raiders, as well. I have ever found them to be knowledgeable and cautious companions-at-arms. When a Sister of Silence rides into a flood without gauging her depths, I know that something is badly amiss. I stood and hailed them as they came dripping up the near side of the flood."

Speaker was leaning forward, her black eyes intent upon the trader. Lehnik found himself tense, his hands clenched in his lap.

Flattered at such rapt attention, the dealer went on. "They were glad enough to stop for a moment beside my fire to dry themselves. I had dried meat, too, and they drank from my wine-skin. When I

51

asked them about matters beyond the ford, the leader looked toward Garrouche and made the sign of danger. She raised three fingers, which I know means great emphasis.

"I understood then that something really bad was happening there, so I asked if they were headed toward Chelos and the Council. She nodded, and made the sign for great haste. Then she made a third sign. This one." His flattened hand swept across his left palm.

The watching Sisters gasped, and he nodded. "Yes. Invasion by an army. You may imagine how quickly I turned my stock in their tracks and made for the nearest town as fast as possible. There was a troop of militia there, and I told them what I had seen and what the riders had signaled.

"They took my mounts, without payment but with my blessing. Good men! They headed directly for Kell-ford, but I fear that must have been the group wiped out to the last man when Garrouche swept across the river." He settled onto one elbow and sighed.

"Now I wait for word of the war. There is no use gathering strings of mounts, just to have them commandeered by the militia, and I am not so fond of taking orders that I intend to join unless it's necessary. Still, I am in fear for my country. I felt that word from an eyewitness might be of value to the Council.

"Who knows if those three Sisters made it to Chelos? The invaders were almost upon their heels, and there are, I feel certain, infiltrators who had entered our lands beforehand."

Speaker took his leathery hand in both her gloved ones. She traced upon his knuckles the line of hills rising to the east. At his fingertips she indicated the mountains. Pointing to a spot near his midmost knuckle, she looked into his eyes and nodded decisively. Then she took from her robe a tablet and a writing stick, with which she scribbled something onto the paper.

She offered that to the horse dealer, who took it and examined the writing. "Ah," he said. "Mayhap there is something I can do that is neither gathering mounts nor soldiering and taking orders. I will go to your House and put myself at their service. I'll not have to take any strange oath or cut out my tongue?" He was only half joking.

Speaker's rich laugh filled the room. Then she rose and looked at Lehnik. He, too, rose and put a generous payment onto the table. They left at once to ready their horses for travel, for there was no time for resting now. If Garrouche had been in the hills two days ago, then the forces of the invaders were even now too near Chelos for comfort.

They pushed hard up the road leading northward. The horses, rested and generously fed and watered, were filled with energy as they trotted along the road. The stream that meandered alongside the track was convenient, for it offered water for the beasts when they might grow thirsty again.

It had been afternoon by the time they left the Inn of the Middle Way. In the wide, flat lands, the sky remained light for a long while after sunset, and the Sisters kept moving in the twilight, though they rested their mounts often.

At last they came near to the point where a stream from the mountains crossed their track to join the larger stream on their right. Speaker gave voice to her thought. "The Venn has cut deeply through the plain ahead. The ford is dark, even by day, and at night the crossing would be perilous. Not only will the animals have trouble seeing where they put their feet, but there may be danger from any who might watch the ford to stop just such messengers as we."

Lehnik grunted. He had long since had occasion to regret the gorge that cut crossed this road. More than once, during the campaigning of Krohm's troop, they had found bandits lying there in ambush. Nature had never made a more likely spot for that sort of activity.

Now their beasts were weary, and even the riders were ready to ease their sore bottoms and their cramped muscles. Some distance from the tall rocks marking the downslope to the cut, they left the road and went down the gentle slope to the tree-studded verge of the stream they had followed.

In the grassy space sheltered by a shrub-grown bank, they loosed the bits of the mounts and the surcingle of the pack animal. The creatures immediately began to crop the tall spring grass, while their riders crouched beside the water. There they munched dried fruits as they stared northward toward the confluence of the streams.

Though the bank curved to hide the joining of the waters, Lehnik knew the point at which the larger stream entered the deep crevasse formed by the united rivers. On the west side a deep canyon marked the course of the Venn, but to the east rolling country swept down to a bluff that overlooked the higher edge of the Altvenn.

What rule dictated that one must travel only by a road? Lehnik lifted an arm against the starred sky and gestured toward the dark bulk that was the other stream-bank. Speaker turned her white-swathed head to follow. When she turned back to face him, he saw her nod.

They rose and tightened the trappings of the horses and reset the packs. Wading ahead of the animals, Lehnik and Speaker moved into the water, first waist-deep and then shoulder-deep, their white robes billowing on the ripples. The horses snorted, following on short reins, as the Sisters tested out the current and the footing.

At midstream the bottom fell away, and the two swam beside their mounts, holding to the saddle straps. The current bore them along the course for several yards, but at last they managed to cross the channel and to find footing again on the other side.

They waded out of the stream onto a narrow beach. Before them was a dark bluff, its contour broken by a game trail that slanted down in a pale line toward the water. In a few moments, they found themselves out on the open grasslands again, with nothing ahead except plains and the broken country beside the Altvenn.

They said nothing else. Plodding ahead of their tired horses, they moved northward, keeping their gazes on the cut that grew blacker as the night went on.

CHAPTER SEVEN

Lehnik led his horse and the pack animal out onto the grassland lying alongside the confluence of the streams, and Speaker followed. If anyone was watching the road where it crossed at the ford, the pale spring grasses might show motion that could be detected by such a watcher, so they did not go far into the flat country but stuck to the hillocks that edged the river. The scrubby growth there was a good screen to conceal their movements from detection.

It was a night with polished black sky studded with entirely too many stars. Their tenuous light made the passage less than secure, for if anyone did watch they might see the shift and shine of leaves in the starlight.

Pausing in a cup of small trees, Speaker made a sign, and Lehnik slipped his robe over his head, turned it inside out, and put it on again with the dark blue lining on the outside. Speaker, close as she was, all but disappeared when her robe was in place, and, cloaked so, they were almost invisible even to each other.

Fortunately, their horses were dark, one a roan, the other two chestnut; no white patches would flash a signal to lookouts above. Keeping low, they led the animals forward, allowing them time to choose their footing carefully.

Lehnik glanced often at the dark bluff above them. He kept a hand on the cheek-strap of his roan, to be ready if the animal should try to whinny. More than once he had known soldiers' mounts to betray a sortie, and he did not intend to allow that to happen now.

He knew better than to tap Speaker's shoulder in warning. She stood at the peak of her Order, and she knew more than he about silence and secrecy when approaching a possible enemy.

His watchfulness was rewarded, for at last there was a hint of motion against the skyline. He imitated the burbling call of a grass warbler, and Speaker halted and waited for him to draw even with her.

He pointed. Her nod was immediate, and he thought that she, too, must have caught that quick blur of movement. She motioned toward an upthrust boulder rising from the ground some distance ahead of them, and they made their quiet way there as quickly as possible.

Sheltered behind its black bulk, they put their heads close together. In the darkness hand signals were useless, and it was time to use words.

"Probably a small group," Lehnik said. "It doesn't take many to hold this ford or to ambush unsuspecting travelers making the crossing. I think we can go around them here, keeping to the grassland and the bushes. Once we pass the joining of the streams, the land is very rough and dangerous, but if we rest the horses well before we set out they should be able to make it."

"What if they have set watchers out in the plain?" she murmured.

"I doubt it. But it is a possibility," he admitted.

Her soft voice sounded again, and he bent to hear. "They would not expect to be attacked from behind, now would they?" she asked. "Particularly if we approached up the steep slope from the river? The Sisters the horse dealer met may have died there. They may have suffered some delay and still come behind us. Should we not clean out this nest of vipers as we pass by?" Her velvety voice went still.

Lehnik chuckled softly. "Why did I waste so much of my life at soldiering, when I could have taken my training in your House? Of course. We are in perfect position to attack those watching the ford. They cannot suspect we are here, and it is no great feat to cross the river, even in flood. I agree. We should remove those watchers—and now I feel certain they are there—from the main artery running north and south through Trans-Kell."

They picketed their mounts in the shelter of the boulder, out of sight of anyone higher on the bluffs. Once they were fitted with nosebags holding grain they would be quiet and content until their riders returned.

Then the Sisters peeled off their long robes and veils, standing in tunics and light breeches in the spring breeze. They rubbed soil well into the light colored stuff and onto Lehnik's pale skin, hiding anything that might show in the starlight.

Lehnik soft-footed it along a game path that went toward the river, which they could hear grumbling along its course, moving rocks that had fallen from the cliffs above or had been cut free from the banks by the flood waters. Speaker went ahead of him, for she had told him the Sisters had mapped every inch of this country.

"Every Sister carries within her mind a key that will bring to mind the map for each area of Trans-Kell. At need she will think of the proper key and enable herself to picture every rock, every canyon, every patch of trees in her path."

"Why did I not have such training?" asked Lehnik.

"That will come, but there has not yet been time for it. This invasion interrupted your training before it was complete."

He swallowed hard. "Then why did you choose me to come with you? Surely, half trained, I cannot be nearly as useful to you as a fully trained Sister might be."

She laughed. "You have campaigned all across Trans-Kell. You know the officers of the different troops of militia, as well as the men. The innkeepers and farm holders and blacksmiths from one end of this country to the other are names and faces to you. That is a valuable matter, and no Sister can claim such knowledge.

"Though we pass people in the course of our errands, we cannot talk with them and get to know their minds and understand their attitudes and opinions. While none who knew you before will recognize you as a Sister, a time will come, I am sure, when your knowledge of those we meet will serve us well."

Climbing the bluff, still following her lead, he found himself thinking of her words. He could understand her reasoning. Krohm, himself, had used Lehnik's knowledge of the common folk among whom the troops moved, more than once. Speaker was using the same techniques that his old commander had, and that raised her even higher in his esteem.

He saw, as they proceeded, that she must indeed carry a chart inside her mind. She scrambled down a runnel he thought must be a channel for water running down from the higher levels of the grassy country. Wild animals had worn it into a serviceable trail. From the dung, he thought they must be the native sheep or the three-horned deer that grazed in the grassland.

By day the track would hardly have been visible. By night, only one with a Sister's training could possibly have found it. At the bottom was a narrow shelf thrusting out into the water of the Altvenn. Just below that point, a boil of ripples in the starlight showed the spot at which the Venn poured into the main current.

The noise was startling, trapped as it was in the deep cut. It echoed back from the cliffs to the west, too, seeming to surround the stalkers.

High above them a ribbon of stars marked the top of the cut through which the road ran, where figures were now moving. Were they changing pickets? The two Sisters lay flat against a boulder and waited for many long heartbeats for some indication that those above had seen them.

No signal, no cry indicated that. No more motion crossed the skyline, and no sound other than the pounding of the waters reached Lehnik's ears.

He dreaded that crossing of the river. He had crossed many streams in his career, and always the possibility of drowning loomed frighteningly in his mind. But he had learned control in two hard schools, and he tied his boots to his belt, fastened the loose legs of his breeches tightly about his calves so they would not entangle him as he swam toward a chain of stones some half a bowshot between the little beach and the farther shore.

Before he could enter the chilly water, Speaker touched his arm. "There is a better way," she whispered.

He started. Surely he could not have heard such a soft sound in the turmoil filling this place, but her hand pushed him down to sit on the pebbly strip. He could see her dark shape against the star-spangled current. She was leaning forward, and there was something in her right hand.

There came a vicious *schwipp!* of sound, audible even above the noise of the waters. She bent to catch his hand. As he rose, she led him forward and pushed his hand outward. He touched a thin line that seemed be strung tightly across the river.

He leaned to run his fingers along that length. It was continuous. In some way she had managed to send this strong, slender cable over the river, probably by some means brought up from the store left by the lost star-farers.

Grateful to be spared the swim, he checked his long knife in its sheath against his leg, his dagger in the sash that wound in many turns about his waist. He fingered the strangling cord pouch that hung about his neck, and he could hear Speaker checking her own weapons.

She waded into the stream, her muddied garments disappearing at once. The tone of the current changed subtly as the water moved about her body, and he could tell how far she had gone by the sound it made.

When that note returned to normal, he reached to touch the cord. Then he set his bare foot in the stream and entrusted himself to the water and the slender cord.

He could feel the snow waters at the head of the Venn in the chill of the river. To swim here would have been dangerous. Perhaps fatal. But the line was firm under his hands, and he tugged himself along as quickly as possible. Suddenly a hand grasped his tunic at the shoulder and pulled.

He found himself in a calm eddy behind a rock on the other side of the river. Moving through the darkness, he followed the lead of the Sister to find another tiny strip of beach along the base of the cliff. Speaker went along it as silently and quickly as if she could see, but he found himself overly cautious.

They were climbing. Who knew what cauldron of troubled water and sharp rock might lie below this narrow track?

At last his companion paused. Her touch brought him up beside her, and she set his hands into a crack running upward like some open-sided chimney. This would be the path to the top, he guessed, unsuspected by any who might watch above.

She was gone from his side, and he heard the whisper of her feet against the stone. She was climbing the sheer face of the cliff along that narrow cranny.

Grit and small pebbles fell occasionally, loosed by her movements. When the soft rain lessened, Lehnik set his back against one wall of the niche and his knees against the other. His own climb began, and it was a long one. He emerged, bruised and sore, into a chill wind that knifed across the top of the cliff.

Speaker's hand touched his shoulder to keep him lying flat as soon as he was clear of the crack. Fingers on his jaw told him to turn his head. From his low position he could see the dark shape of a man silhouetted against the stars.

The watcher was staring away toward the east. His stance was easy, not alert. Lehnik nodded, and Speaker's hand was gone.

As he wriggled forward on the cliff top he heard a sound, half sigh, half grunt, and he knew this first watcher was dead. He crawled on to the spot where the man had stood. Speaker was waiting.

"You are certain that these are our enemies?" Lehnik asked almost soundlessly. He was suddenly and bitterly aware that their own troops might have set a watch here.

"Garrouche," she breathed into his ear. She set into his hand a square medallion, and he felt it over.

His fingers lingered over the raised figure of a torch set into a triangle. It was, without doubt, the insignia of the Elector of Garrouche.

He tucked it into his sash and moved on elbows and belly toward a boss of rock, around which he peered. This marked the turning of the path atop the cliff. A sharp click brought him up short. Nothing natural had made that sound. Another man must be positioned along this part of the ragged edge of the bluff. Where?

He crept around the bend and curled himself into a notch, where three stones lay together to form a tiny shelter. Speaker drew back to admit him into the small space and sat straight, her legs folded under her. He could see her severe profile against the lighter sky as she concentrated upon sensing the presence of any enemies.

Yet it was Lehnik who located them. Something inside him woke, there on the height, and he knew, without understanding how, that the second man was standing sheltered from the wind in a niche just a few yards farther along the path. He reached to touch Speaker's arm and pointed. The Sister nodded, and he saw the glint of her white teeth against her ebony face.

Lehnik knew stalking better than anything else. For years his life had depended upon his expertise at dispatching unwanted scouts, skulkers, or those hidden in ambush. Almost without conscious thought, he wriggled silently toward the spot he had chosen, which was just short of the place where he sensed the presence of the lookout. Lehnik stood and readied his strangling cord.

With one toe he scritched two pebbles against each other. The man came out of hiding with a rush, but Lehnik was poised, waiting for him. The cord looped effortlessly around the watcher's neck. One sharp twist finished the task. The sharp tang of ammonia fouled the night air, and Lehnik knew his victim was dead.

Speaker appeared, a dim shape in the darkness, and pointed along the path. He followed her to a spot at which she gestured downward. At almost the same moment, she disappeared from sight.

He could see six men waiting at the ford. They had built a fire in a sheltered nook that was invisible from the road. Three warmed themselves by the blaze while the rest kept watch from square blocks of stone flanking the first descent to the water.

Lehnik wondered what sort of officers were trained in Garrouche, for it was stupid to have any fire at all, however sheltered, when you planned an ambush. Or was that scene below the bait in some sort of trap, set for unexpected flankers who might climb from the river?

He tilted his head toward the spot where three dark shapes showed against the leaping flames. Speaker shook her head and pointed toward the approach to the ford. He smiled. Again their minds were running in the same track.

There would be passwords or signals among those guarding this spot, so the two waited while the stars moved placidly overhead. At last Speaker located the position of the man atop the right hand boulder. She flowed down the stone and disappeared among the tumbled debris about the foot of the outcrop.

Lehnik spotted another man who lay behind a snag of rock on the other flank-stone. There should be still a third. Probably a six-man platoon had been left there, together with the two lookouts above. Only seven were accounted for, so far. There should, by the very orderly nature of soldiering, be an eighth man. Something about odd numbers seemed to trouble those who practiced warfare.

There was motion, very slight, almost imperceptible, below and to his right. Then he saw the man, who had positioned himself in a nest of rocks by the water's edge. Now Lehnik, too, flowed down the rocky way to slither into the debris. He found a way to reach the water and then moved up the stream, covered by the rush of the Venn. His prey could not see the river from his position, for he had been placed to watch the road.

That was his undoing. He died silently, much to Lehnik's relief.

Now it was time to see to the man on the flank-stone, but Speaker had been there already, after eliminating the other watcher. She met her companion on the road as he turned toward that direction. There remained only those beside the fire.

Without words, the two parted, one moving up into the needle-like formations worn into the streamward face of the river gorge. The other clambered over the top of the cliff.

Their enemies lay there, two dozing, the third watching. Noise was no longer a factor because of the rush of water, and the Sisters leaped from convenient heights upon their prey. Long knives were at the ready, and two men went into their hereafter instantly. The third they kept for questioning, for he wore the horn-and-star insignia of an officer.

They did not hold him at the ford, however. They took him across the river, up the game path, and into the plain to the spot where the horses waited. There they tied their captive tightly and lay down for a couple of hours of much needed sleep.

CHAPTER EIGHT

Lehnik had not intended to sleep deeply. Dozing for a couple of hours, one ear against the ground, had been his plan, but he woke suddenly, knowing that he had not remained alert. Even Speaker was still lying still, and he rolled out of his blanket to glance toward their prisoner.

But the officer had not escaped. He still lay motionless, his bindings secure though not painful. That relieved Lehnik. He hadn't entirely failed in his trust.

The sun was well above the horizon as the two Sisters rolled their blankets, tied them onto their saddles, and sidled along the sheltering boulder until Lehnik could see the height up which they had climbed the night before. There was no movement there at all, though surely if relief had been sent to the watchers those who found them dead or missing would have been buzzing like disturbed bees.

But Lehnik almost could make out one limp shape lying on the stone ledge high above. It was illusion, of course, for he knew just where to look. The dark speck there could be anything, stone or shadow. The dark carrion birds that already circled high above were not illusions, however, and they would betray the night's activities to anyone who watched from afar.

Speaker, also gazing upward, turned to him and gestured toward the north. Lehnik helped her lift the prisoner across her mount's crupper, where his wiry bulk would pose no burden for the powerful roan. Tall as she was, Speaker was very slender and light of bone. Carrying double would not trouble the horse.

In moments they were galloping along the edge of the grass-land, where it began sloping down toward the stream. They set as much distance as possible between themselves and the betraying scavengers who were still gathering about the dead at the ford.

Without discussing it, they avoided the road entirely, though that meant traveling through the broken and stream-cut country north of the junction of the Venn and the Alt-Venn. Lehnik knew from old experience that this was best, for if the ford was watched, so also would be the road north. Garrouche would be more than interested in this approach to Chelos.

He had never, of course, crossed the Crumpled Plain. No officer in his senses would try moving any considerable numbers over that terrible terrain. An army had to travel by road, if it was to move its supply wagons and extra mounts without losing them.

That meant that he and Speaker must cross the plain. If Garrouche moved between them and the capital city, the forces would be along the traveled way. But the journey would have been far easier afoot and alone than it would be caring for their horses. Steeps and scree that were passable for a human foot were hellish for hooves.

Even after they passed the plain, Lehnik knew that they must travel at top speed to reach their goal. And if the prisoner was to accompany them to those capable of questioning him to good purpose, he must be tied on the roan. That would make the animal's balance come into question, for it would have to be blindfolded and led down declivities that would have sent it into hysteria, if the horse could see.

The journey was even more difficult than he had thought. Staggering through pocked stretches of shale, climbing long shelving slopes of rotten sandstone, descending into broken canyons of thin soil and rubble, it tried the Sisters as much as it did their beasts. The two begrudged every moment spent in maneuvering the laden horses through the obstacles, but both knew that they must have the animals, once they reached the smooth grass covering the farther reaches of the plain.

Coming out of the badlands at last, they rejoiced to find the plain green and rolling ahead of them. Two days lost struggling in the Crumpled Plain could be made up quickly, once the mounts were rested.

Another day, riding and walking and resting, a night, with brief sleep snatched grudgingly, saw them at the upper edge of the grasslands. They topped a low rise at last and found themselves looking down on Chelos.

It was mid-day, and the sea beyond the city glinted like a million silver coins beneath the spring sun. The bay was wide and deep, and one arm of land arched to the north and east, curving to protect the anchorage.

It was a familiar sight. Lehnik had approached his home city from every possible direction as he served the militia commanded by Krohm. He had often been sent with messages to the Council, coming from every direction except by sea.

A faint track led through the meadow opening before them, where cattle and goats and sheep grazed. Nearby farms served the most basic needs of the inhabitants of Chelos, and this rich soil made that easy.

Speaker led the way forward, her roan nudging stray animals out of its way as they proceeded. In the distance there was the pale gleam of the road, whose windings they had avoided by taking the harder way.

Lehnik knew there would be sentries set in the watchtowers of the city, and he raised his arms and signaled energetically, using the last series of gestures he had learned before leaving the militia. It was just as well that those understand that these were no enemies but messengers with important news.

Before the pair had crossed half the meadow, a file of horsemen was moving out from the line of buildings and screen-walls ahead. As they drew nearer, Lehnik had to use all his control to keep from shouting a greeting.

He did remember in time that he was no longer Lehnik Avarien, Master of Horse. He was now an anonymous Sister of Silence, and he was forbidden to hail Benthe, the sergeant of the Council Guard, no matter how he longed to. That would betray his identity and the fact that he was a man. No matter how many years of friendship might lie between him and the sergeant, it must be forgotten for the present.

Speaker kicked her mount into a brisk trot as they approached. She drew rein just short of those who had come to meet them. "Speaker of the House of Silent Women!" she called. "To meet with the Council at once!"

Lehnik could see the shock on the old sergeant's face at being addressed in words by one whom he had believed was mute. However, the sergeant did not allow that to betray him into a breach of polite procedure. He turned the troop in obedience to Speaker's white-gloved hand and followed the newcomers back toward the city.

For most of its circumference, Chelos was unwalled, and its growth had been random and undisciplined. It sprawled along the great curve of the bay, to right and to left. It straggled inland for considerable distance. Yet though no central plan seemed to have been set in its design, there was grace and proportion to the shape of the city.

The houses, different as they were, blended well with each other in color and design. Large stone buildings housing the businesses of merchants, sea-traders, and the university made an attractive pattern against the sea and the sky.

At the point where roads arriving from south, east, and west met the broad avenue running down to the docks and wharves, there was a circle of exquisitely cut stone blocks. In the middle of its arc stood a low building, domed pleasingly and made of white sandstone. It was decorated with low reliefs carved to show parts of the history of Halash.

As the mounted group drew near the circle, the wide doors of the Chamber of the Council swung open, and Lehnik saw three Councilors come out onto the low steps. They stood at the top of the fan of steps, waiting serenely as the Sisters dismounted and the sergeant cut loose the prisoner and took him in charge.

A trooper led away the horses, but Speaker was already hurrying up the steps toward those waiting at their top. Her hands moved in a blur of motion too quick for Lehnik to interpret. Yet even deciphering the sign language as slowly as he still must, he caught hints of meaning. At her heels, he followed the Councilors back into the dimness of their Chamber.

The interior was arranged in a great circle of benches, spaced around an open area at the center. Every bench held its complement of members, whose hushed murmurs of surprise quieted as the doors closed behind the newcomers.

Speaker made her way at once to a cushioned bench in the center of the circle, where she stood, free to face any portion of her audience she might need to address. Lehnik, following her still, sat on one end of the bench at her gesture.

A scuffle of feet announced the arrival of the two troopers who supported the unwilling shape of the prisoner. They set him on a stool and fastened a metal cuff, attached to a short length of chain, about his ankle. Then they turned with military precision and left the round chamber through a lesser door.

Only when that door was closed behind them did Speaker make it clear that she was ready to begin. A tall man rose from his bench facing her. He bent his neck in greeting.

"Welcome to those from the House of Silence. Our need is great, and every help possible is to be welcomed, also."

Lehnik knew well the ritual for approaching the Council, but Speaker ignored all the rules of conduct. Instead, she raised both hands and removed her veil, along with her cloak, now soiled and dusty and stained with rusted traces of old blood.

Her ebony face gleamed in the diffused light falling through the crystal dome as she spoke. "Have three Sisters out of Garrouche come to you within the past weeks?" she asked abruptly.

The leader glanced about at his peers, his expression puzzled. Then he shook his head. "No. What has come to us out of Garrouche is another matter entirely. We are invaded by forces that strike and run, slashing and harrying our armies, burning towns and farms, destroying what they can and taking away what is portable.

"Our armies are weary and frustrated. These are no ordinary raids, and we have not been able to come to grips with any large force in a straightforward battle. We are being bled to death without making any dent in the forces we are facing."

"Four days ago," said the Speaker, "we met a horse dealer at the Inn of the Middle Way. He was camped, he told us, at Kell-Ford when those three Sisters crossed out of Garrouche, moving into the flood without checking their depths. They told him that an army was at their heels, and they were riding to warn Chelos that it was set to invade us."

There came a low murmur, a rustling of moving bodies and shifting garments from the listeners. Speaker went on without pausing. "He hurried to the nearest town and informed the militia. They took his string of fresh mounts and rode out to confront the invaders. Later he heard of a troop that died to the last man in defending Kell-Ford. He thought it might be those men. Have you had word of such an occurrence?"

The Councilor nodded. "That word was brought by Krohm himself, when he came to ask for fresh men and horses. We sent with him what we could spare, but we kept back several detachments to send to the aid of any settlements needing help. We have lost three towns along the hills west of the Kell, and even now the city is crowded with people seeking refuge from the invaders."

Speaker looked around her, her black eyes seeming to probe deeply into the faces of the Councilors. When she spoke it was in a tone both sad and determined.

"We bring worse news yet. Some of you have been trained for your duties in the House from which I have come. You will understand too well the thing that I will say. Those not trained so may find it hard to understand the seriousness of this news. The Elector of Garrouche has breached the House of Silence serving his country."

A collective gasp went around the circle of benches. Lehnik felt the impact of their shock as they heard this news. The House provided the stability, the emotional anchors that held the governments of the countries on Halash on course.

As well, they provided help for those who were overcome by catastrophes, either natural or otherwise. All the healers were trained by the Sisterhood, as well as most of the teachers in the schools.

"Still there is worse," Speaker said. "He filched from their Archives the weapons systems left in our care by the ancestors."

There came a low outcry from a few throats. The rest looked puzzled, and one stood to address the Speaker. "Weaponry? Belonging to our ancestors?" she asked, looking bewildered. "There is no history of unusual weaponry, or at least not that I learned about. I spent years at University, and I never heard anything about such a thing. Explain yourself, Sister."

She sighed. "You know that our ancestors who first arrived on this world came here on ships moving through space. Consider the knowledge of physics such a journey implies!

"Much of the weaponry in our charge makes use of the more esoteric laws of physics. Think about it. Even the flight of an arrow or the trajectory of a flung stone depends upon physical laws that must be understood, instinctively if not theoretically, if the missile is to reach its goal."

Heads nodded around the circle, considering her words. She drew a deep breath and continued, "Our kind brought with them, and you have not been taught this at University, a large number of devices that possess great power and are incredibly dangerous. These were to be used in subduing worlds our ancestors hoped we would discover and conquer. We were to use their techniques, building more ships in order to visit and colonize worlds still farther from the source of our kind.

"Those devices, weapons, systems are capable of destroying this planet totally, along with every living person and creature living on its surface. Along with those are other techniques and systems capable of healing those who are better allowed to die." Her tone was now even sadder.

"The predecessors of the present Sisters of Silence were leaders of the earliest colonists, who were given the responsibility for preserving those weapons, in order to dispense or withhold them, whatever their best judgment decided. They understood, once they had taken root here on Halash, that there was more danger inherent in many of the things in their charge than any possible help or usefulness.

"We are prone to squabbles and wars and other disagreements, which often turn into emotional and physical combat. If one side of such quarreling groups should possess such terrible weapons, they could wreak havoc against their opponents. This is a relatively young society, and we might well be destroyed or sent back to the level of beasts."

The leader of the Council looked as if he might weep, and his hands, clasped before him, flexed and relaxed, flexed and relaxed. Lehnik knew this was no fresh news to the fellow.

"It was agreed among our more ancient predecessors that those weapons would be preserved according to the directive, but they would never be dispensed to the people of Halash. Only if there was peril threatened from beyond our own skies would those awful potentialities be unloosed by those trained in their uses."

The Council, as Lehnik glanced around the circle, looked stunned. One of those nearest said, "They took it upon themselves to deny such power...," but Speaker shook her head.

"Not they. We. The discipline they created is the one we follow to this day. We who love knowledge and have the capacity to deny our own natures are entrusted with that terrible responsibility. If we had not kept our trust, there would probably be none of our kind left on Halash. The world itself might be shattered into segments hurtling through the sky." She frowned, and the leader himself shrank before her expression.

"Now one who has not learned control, who cannot deny his short-term desires, possesses a part of those weapons left by the starfarers. He wants nothing except power over his fellows, and he has the key to that power within his grasp."

The elderly woman who had spoken turned pale, seeming to shrink within her blue robe. "Then we can expect only disaster to follow? We cannot win the war the invaders bring to our doorsteps?"

Speaker stood taller, straighter. "Not quite. The Elector, though he is unwise, self-willed, unable to understand what it is he has seized, is not a fool. He saw, once he realized what he had in his hands, that these weapons are far too dangerous to use without training.

"So far he has not used them against us. We cannot detect any experimental use of them in his own country. He is, at this time, using ordinary troops and tactics, so as to avoid accidental disaster connected with those weapons. But one who died after delivering the message told me that he *will* use them. If he fails to conquer us by normal means, he will unleash catastrophe upon us and other neighbors whose lands he covets."

One of the Councilors rose to his feet. "Then we must ask the Sisters to release the weapons held in the House in Trans-Kell. Surely, if it means the survival of our nation, that will be justified."

Speaker's straight form seemed to droop. Lehnik rose and stood beside her, setting his hand on her shoulder and lending her his strength. He knew the despair in her heart, for it touched his own, as well.

"That is a question I have debated with my Sisters and also inside my own mind," she said. "It is the thing we have come to the Council to determine. We do not know and cannot estimate the extent of the damage these things can do. Perhaps if we defend ourselves by using them we will destroy ourselves totally. I think the risk is great and the course may lack wisdom. Do you agree?"

The man sank onto his bench, pale to the jowls. He shook his head slowly. Most of the other Councilors did the same.

"Has no study been done to learn about these matters?" he asked. "Surely as the Sisterhood has been in charge of them since the beginning you should have assigned some of your number to investigate and master them." His tone was sharp with fear.

Speaker sighed. "And what would you have had us neglect in order to do that? There are never enough applicants for the Sisterhood. We are all constantly on call, the Council itself keeping us busy as messengers or secret emissaries or observers. The educators from one end of this land to the other must be taught by us, as must as healers and leaders.

"Why should we have foreseen the need for understanding those things that had been stored away for two thousand years? They were safe in the hands of our own kind, scattered all over this great continent. We have never misused them and never would.

"From end to end, side to side of this great continent that is the landmass of our world, everything has been safe, secure, and controlled, even in the frequent conflicts between nations. Who would ever have dreamed that one day our kind would produce a man mad enough to consider breaching a House of Silence?"

Another Councilor rose from her chair, her frail body shaking with the force of her emotion. "There has to be some instruction...

some direction written that can inform us of the powers and uses of these devices," she said.

"Probably, among the mountains of archives in the Houses on Halash, there are such instructions," Speaker agreed. "But it would take generations to pore through them, and the mechanisms that our ancestors used to read them are hidden among all those others. We do not know which would work and which are other and more dangerous things."

Speaker turned around the circle, letting her gaze fall upon every member of the Council. "You know—who could possibly know better?—that very few seek to live the disciplined life we of the Sisterhood offer. Those of you who know that best had the opportunity to embrace the Order when your education was completed.

"Yet now you are here, which proves that you feel for your country the concern we tried to instill in you. But it also proves that you could not find it in your hearts to relinquish all the matters humankind finds so dear and necessary.

"Do you wonder that even fewer of those who are *not* educated by us choose to join us? Ours is not an easy life, yet it is natural and comfortable for some. For a very few. Do not blame us for faults caused only by our lack of numbers."

Another woman rose, tall and thin and middle-aged, her bony frame seeming too slender to hold her upright. "You are saying there is no way in which we can utilize those weapons in your hands, even for our own defense, without risking destruction?" Her voice was low and firm, her tone that of a good commander, setting matters straight and clear before a campaign.

"That is what I am saying."

"Then we must contrive to prevent the Elector from using them. In that, I can think of none who might succeed except the Sisterhood. Can you find among your number some who are willing to go into Garrouche, into the very stronghold of the Elector, and to destroy his armory?" She looked stern, forbidding, but Lehnik found himself cheering her silently.

Speaker smiled, her teeth bright against her dark face. "Carrolia, I have heard that you think clearly and to good effect, for all these years since you completed our school and departed. Perhaps you may be the single member of this group who would have chosen the Life, if your health had allowed it. Minds such as yours are valuable to us all."

Her nod was crisp and confident. "We will find many who will volunteer, more than we need. Any would be glad to go, but few will be needed. For the one thing we know certainly is a way to destroy any cache of such weaponry, wherever it is and no matter how it is housed."

She turned toward Lehnik. "This is a new Sister, less than fully trained, yet completely competent for such work. I have had that demonstrated to me over the past days. How many do you believe we will need to go, Sister Lehnik?"

Surprised, Lehnik also felt a great warmth spread through him as he realized that she had chosen him first. His mind had already been busy with the question since the Councilor finished stating it.

"Not more than four," he said. "Followed, at an interval of two days, by four more, as a precaution against disaster befalling the first group. We will need every device from the old store that is in use—I have seen one such already. Things that will help us cross rough country, to ford streams in flood, to climb mountains quickly and without waste of time will be of great value. These, if there are others, should be harmless and will lend us the speed we will need."

"There are many small items, conveniences rather than weapons, that will make the journey faster," Speaker said. She turned to survey the Council once again.

"I will choose from the Sisterhood gathered here in Chelos, for we cannot spare the time to summon any from our own House. Your House in Chelos possesses many such tools that may speed the journey to the Elector's stronghold.

"If any of you have objections or suggestions, tell me now. There is no time for deliberations or preparations. I shall send Sister Lehnik in the first group. She may choose one of her companions, and I will choose the other pair. They will leave soon, but if no one knows the hour, nobody can betray us."

The first Councilor, who had greeted them, now rose. His long face was grim and shocked, but he held out his hands to the Sisters in a gesture of good will and farewell. "As always," he said, "we are grateful for your help. We wish you well. All our efforts will be bent toward holding Trans-Kell against the invaders, while you seek to remove the poison from the serpent's sting."

Speaker bowed. Lehnik bent his knee as well and followed her from the chamber, at whose door Benthe stood guard. As Lehnik passed him, the sergeant whispered, "Is this truly the Lehnik I have known for so long? You are evidently one with the Sisters of Silence, but I cannot understand how that can be."

Speaker turned to him and set her finger across his lips. "Meet with us," she murmured, "at the House of our Order on the Street of the Jewelcutters, once your watch is done. I will answer all your questions at that time. For now, keep a still tongue and do not mention the Lehnik you knew."

Benthe stared at her. Then he nodded and took up his rigid stance beside the door. Though Speaker moved away at once, Lehnik felt that she must have read the burly sergeant to the centers of his bones and the deeps of his spirit, in that brief instant of contact.

Fresh horses waited for them outside the domed chamber. Speaker took the reins of one from the boy who held them and Lehnik those of the other. He mounted and rode after her toward the street she had mentioned, which was in the oldest part of the city, next to the bay and near the docks.

Over their heads the white and pale blue sea birds squawked and wheeled, as they rode toward the water. The streets were crowded, but a path appeared before them as they entered each jog of the crooked ways, and those they passed made the sign of respect due to the Sisters of Silence.

This House of Silence was no stronghold, as was its mother house. Set directly on the street, its bulk looming against warehouses beyond it, this place was a stopping point for any of the Sisterhood who had business in Chelos. Its own Sisters taught and tended the sick and kept a watchful eye on the Council.

The gate leading through the bulk of the hollow square into the courtyard the House enclosed stood open. Lehnik noted with dismay that it seemed not to have been shut in decades, so rusted were its hinges. As they rode into the courtyard, he could see that the great leaves had settled solidly onto the cobblestones. An invading enemy would rush in without hindrance.

The past generations of security were now gone, he knew as he dismounted, and Lehnik determined to mention the state of the gates to the Sister in charge of the House. As the horses were led away, he moved after Speaker up the short flight of steps and in at the arched doorway leading into the back of the quadrangle.

Speaker had told him, as they traveled, that here there were only some fifty Sisters, and most of those were in constant motion, serving as couriers for the Council. Coming and going, they carried messages to Krohm and his fellow officers who were scattered about the country. Those who dwelled here permanently were the old and infirm, Sisters who had worked their hardest in their youth and now were advisors to those who were younger.

Simple as it was, this House was comfortable, the cubicles furnished with firm pallets, the table set with excellent food. Moving among those who were now taking their meal in the refectory, Lehnik found a place and fell to. He was weary and hungry, after the scanty rations of the past days.

Not long after they completed their meal, Benthe rapped with the ram's head knocker on the door through which they had first entered the House. Speaker led him, along with Lehnik, into a small chamber set aside for private meetings. She gestured, once they were inside, for her companion to unveil himself, allowing his old friend to see his face.

Benthe drew a huge breath, his eyes wide with surprise. "But you are not a woman!" he said, after a long moment.

Lehnik smiled, and Speaker chuckled. "Many of our Sisterhood are not women," she said.

Lehnik added, "I have thought about this for a long while. I believe I have at last determined the reason why we must all be called Sister and thought to be women. Only a man who is secure enough within himself to feel comfortable with being thought a woman by any casual comer is strong enough to learn the discipline we must incorporate into our characters."

As he spoke he knew that at last he had found the proper expression for the truth he had found. "One who must prove himself among men, for bodily strength, quickness of wit, courage in battle is useless to us. He is too busy impressing women or keeping an anxious eye upon his own image."

"But...you are allowed to talk!" Benthe's tone was that of a man whose preconceptions were crumbling about him.

Speaker laughed aloud this time. "We take no oath. Silence allows us the opportunity to use our minds without the hindrance of constant babble. When there is need, we talk aloud. Surely you have noticed that words foment quarrels and misunderstandings. Actions cannot be misunderstood. Words stand in the path of deep thought."

Lehnik wrapped his veil again about his face and added, "Usually we communicate by hand signals or whistles." He offered his gloved right hand to Benthe. "The glove hides hands that might seem too large for a woman."

When Benthe caught at his fingers, Lehnik said, "You are one of the few men I have met in all my years of soldiering who possesses the confidence and self control I see among these new companions. I am told that I may choose one of those who will go with me into Garrouche. If you are willing, I ask that you become the one. Will you come?"

Benthe stared into his eyes, now half hidden by the veil. Then he turned to stare in turn at Speaker. "You would allow it?" he asked. "It is possible to become a Sister, just like that?"

"At need," she said. "I know you by reputation, sergeant. When you met us in the meadow, I thought already that you might make one of the group who must go into Garrouche, whether or not the Council saw fit to sanction it. Carrollia was not the first to plan toward removing the forces of destruction from the hands of the Elector."

She examined his face quietly, her black eyes sharp and quick. "Do you object to going veiled and cloaked, as a Sister must? It will be best if you are thought to be a true Sister, unrecognized as a member of the Council Guard. If the sergeant of the guard should leave with us, it might cause remark."

Benthe loosed Lehnik's hand. "I will go, and gladly, clad as a roving dancer, if necessary. But my officer must give his leave for it."

Speaker nodded. "It is done already. Lehnik can tell you that when we need a soldier, permission is never denied to us. We of the Sisterhood see a bit ahead of circumstances. I wish we could see even farther and more clearly!"

Lehnik, watching those two, found himself wishing the same thing. This was going to be a difficult and dangerous task they undertook, and there was no guarantee of success, whatever they might try.

CHAPTER NINE

Speaker's words had been no exaggeration, when she mentioned they would leave soon. Though Lehnik was assigned to a quiet cubicle and managed to get a few hours of sleep, when he woke the arrangements for his journey were all but completed. The Sister who called for him led him back into the room where he had last seen Benthe.

There Speaker was waiting. "Sister," she greeted him, "these will be your traveling companions on this mission. Sister Kerrill...." The tall square figure standing by the door bent a white-swathed head in acknowledgment—"...and Sister Sallek."

The short, slender Sister offered her hand, as Lehnik made the sign of greeting. When he took her fingers in his own, he found it small-boned and fragile in the anonymous white glove. A woman, then. But those fingers gripped his with surprising strength, and he knew this was a trained warrior, whatever her sex.

Speaker was saying, "Kerrill is our liaison with the priesthoods of both Trans-Kell and Garrouche. You will find, perhaps, some help among the Brothers, but more peril, we fear."

Lehnik stared questioningly at her, and she bent her proud head, touching her fingers to the veil at her chin. "There has always been friendship and cooperation between the Houses of Silence and the Fraternity of Spiritual Teachers. At one time, long before even our fathers were born, many of those teachers were trained by our Order.

"It has been generations since that was true, but the remnant of the old friendship has remained. Until now." She turned her gaze toward Kerrill.

A deep, masculine voice said, "There has been much strange writing coming from Garrouche in the past year. Philosophies alien to both our orders have sprung into being there. Their priesthood has always maintained a free association with that of our own land, and the dogma that grew up across the Kell has contaminated the thinking of our own Teachers of the Spirit." He shifted uneasily.

"For that reason, there is now a rule that only a male of the Sisters of Silence may communicate with the Fraternity. The teachers have come to believe that women are intrinsically evil, and a land whose affairs are directed in great part by women is an abomination.

"They say our government must be destroyed, to be rebuilt along the lines they espouse. That belief was, of course, shaped in Garrouche, where women are considered lesser beings than the males. The divergence between the Orders can only strengthen the hand of the Elector."

Kerrill folded his large white hands before his robe and stared through the slit in his veiling. "In particular, they point out the Sisters of Silence as the target of their most bitter hatred, among the younger members of the Fraternity. Our Council reveres us and uses our talents and skills to the utmost. That rankles with the young Teachers.

"The people trust us and turn to us in their extremity, and that also rankles, for the Fraternity has never been known for charity or kindness. However, those very Brothers have found it is impossible to indoctrinate any who are outside their order in these lies. Only within their own ranks do they find it possible to nurture hatred of our kind. That rankles most of all."

The big Sister turned to look into Lehnik's eyes. "Not all are contaminated, however. Many adhere secretly to the old teachings, the old ways, recalling generations of cooperation with their Sisters. They will help us now, in our effort. But we must go cautiously as we make contact with any of the Fraternity. Our chance of betrayal there is at least as good as that of finding help among the Order."

Lehnik found he had been holding his breath. He had always been taught reverence for the members of the Fraternity, from his childhood. Since becoming a soldier, however, he had found small opportunity to meet any of that Order, for the Brothers shunned danger and battle.

Now he recalled that they had always been the first to flee from any town threatened by raids. Always they carried away with them the rich ornaments and the other wealth of their houses. If they now preached hatred of those braver than they, it was probably to conceal their own cowardice.

There came a rap at the door. Kerrill opened it to admit a stocky shape that somehow seemed uncomfortable in its concealing white. This had to be Benthe, there was no doubt of it. It would take him some time to become comfortable with his robes and veils.

"The mounts are ready," the sergeant said to Speaker. "Council has provided all needed supplies. The House has put together a pack beast's load of supplies and equipment of unusual kinds. Those should prove useful, they say. If all are now ready, we should be off, for it is well past midnight."

The four travelers turned toward Speaker, who said no word of farewell. Her hands moved gracefully, making the sign that said, "Go quickly and return in safety."

Then they followed Benthe from the room and down a corridor at whose end was a narrow door concealed behind a tapestry. That opened into a cellar, which was stocked with the remnants of the winter's store of dried and preserved foods. It smelled at once musty and fruity, with an overlay of mold and dust.

The group passed through the dark space quickly, for Benthe produced a fireglass, which threw a long beam of white light ahead of them. Swinging sharply around the end of a row of tall shelves, the sergeant ducked into a low cranny. His companions fitted themselves into it as best they could and followed, still. The passage widened, once past its low entrance, to reveal lumpy bags of potatoes and turnips, now rotting and odorous.

Benthe sidestepped the mess to pass along in the space between the heap of vegetables and a wall of crates. Once beyond that he turned again, this time to the right. There they found themselves facing a stone wall.

Kerrill pushed past his fellows and moved to place his hands against the damp sandstone. He felt over it for a moment, while Benthe held the light close to help him see. In a short while there was a gritting sound, together with a whiff of sea water, strong and salty.

A segment of the wall pivoted, grating grit against stone, revealing a dark sliver of opening. Kerrill went through it and the others followed on his heels. Benthe came last of all, his light making strange shadow-patterns run before them. They found themselves in a large cavern that echoed to every whisper of movement.

A chorus of echoing drips told them this was a cave, one of those leading inland from the bay. It was said in Chelos that the earliest inhabitants of the city had sheltered in these caverns until they could build drier and airier quarters aboveground.

There came a whicker, the sound of hoof scraping rock. This was where their mounts waited for them, Lehnik knew, but his thought was interrupted by a quiet voice, almost at his elbow.

"Welcome to the cellar of our House, Sisters," said the voice. "I only regret that we cannot help you openly. However, we must hide our deeds from our own Brothers. Yet we do what we can." The dark-robed brother's tone was sad.

"Now if you will find your horses, I will lead you to a point at which you will be able to ride forth beneath the stars. You will be a long way from the streets of Chelos when you emerge from these tunnels."

Benthe turned his lightglass to help them find their mounts. The stone sparkled with damp, and the Teacher gestured toward the dark huddle of horses.

Lehnik found his own horse among the others. It recognized him and whickered as he took the cheek strap in hand and moved forward after the Brother who led them. Behind, he could hear other hooves, as well as feet moving on damp stone and gravel.

After what seemed hours of walking in darkness, they emerged into a deserted cove. The bay sparkled beneath the stars, and the shoreline was a black blur curving away to the left and the right. A low cliff sheltered this cove from wind, and Lehnik spotted a path, more a groove than anything else, cut into the edge of the cupped depression. That had to be the path they were to take.

"May God go with you," said the Brother. "Now I must leave you. The path to the top of the cliff is there before you, and my prayer accompanies your journey. May you be able to save us all from a fatal folly." His dim shape melted into the darkness of the cave and was gone.

It was too dark to see hand signs. Lehnik whispered into the darkness, "I know where we are. I have traveled this way, though by day. Do you want me to lead?"

A grunt of agreement came to his ears, though he felt certain the Sisters also knew the way they must take. He turned his mount toward the path, where he had ambushed smugglers who were bringing madweed from Horniche.

Krohm had led that foray, which had captured not only the smugglers but also the son of the Hereditary Hierarch of Horniche, who had been in charge of the operation. Under questioning, the young man admitted that his mother intended to enslave the populations of Trans-Kell and Garrouche by use of that weed. It would make her takeover easy, when the time came, for those addicted to the drug were incapable of managing anything, far less a war.

The Council had held the son of the Hierarch, to insure the good behavior of his mother. He probably was still in custody, somewhere in Chelos.

Lehnik's horse found the narrow path leading up the cliff, his hooves scuffling in the sand as he struggled up the declivity. Once out in the open, Lehnik reined him in to wait for the others to join him. Soon all four mounts and the two pack horses stood together in the starlight.

They were well around the eastern arm of the bay, and the lights of Chelos glimmered across the water. But here the stars shone more brightly still, seeming very near as Lehnik led the group along the edge of the cliffs that rose on the seaward edge of Trans-Kell. Inland there were tumbles of sandstone, flung up over the ages by the terrible storms coming in from the sea.

By daylight the horses were weary. The riders, too, were ready to rest, and as dawn moved over the grasslands to the south, the bay to the north, Lehnik looked for a sheltered spot in which to rest and feed the horses. They had been walking almost all night. It was time to give everyone a break from their efforts.

Ahead loomed a high cape, an unusual outthrust of the planet's stony bones that rose through this low and sandy shore. Lehnik knew it marked one side of the mouth of the Kell, which flowed to sea beyond its adamant height. As they approached the headland, the way became thick with stone ridges and patches of granite heaving up amid the sand and pebbles. The beach's dunes were higher than those farther to the west, making cover enough so that no passing ship headed for the harbor would be able to see them moving along the road to Garrouche.

Lehnik pointed ahead and to his right. There a low hill curved out from the flank of the cape, crowned with scrubby trees and thick bushes. Good cover, they all agreed, for their camp.

They settled into a small hollow surrounded by round-leaved corund trees. Their big leaves roofed the spot they chose, sheltering them from the sun. The horses were staked in the hidden cup formed by the curve of the hill and the base of the height, and there tough grass grew abundantly. The animals alternately grazed and rested during the afternoon.

Sleep was begrudged, but they knew they must all rest, and as he drowsed Lehnik pushed from his mind all thought of their prospects for success. When he slept at last, he did not dream.

Before sunrise all were up and readying themselves to travel again. They broke their fast with journey bread and dried fruit, saddled their horses, and set off. With the disturbed state of affairs in the countryside, it was unlikely they would meet any traveler on this least-used route between the neighboring countries.

Lehnik hoped that would be true, for they now must leave the sheltering hillocks and cross the road that swung south of the cape. Climbing the forbidding height was no task for horses or for travelers who were in a hurry. To his relief, the road lay empty as far as could be seen in both directions. They darted across its bare width without any glimpse of a watcher being detected.

They turned at once back toward the coast. Now the Kell spread before them at the widest point it attained in all its course. Contained by the stone of the cape on the west, the waters spread into a maze of marshland on the eastern side of the river. Only where the road had been built up to keep travelers on solid ground was there an easy passage through Kell-marsh, for there stone had been set painfully upon stone to form a long dike with arched sluices to let the water through.

That easy route was now far to the south of them, for Lehnik knew this crucial point would be under surveillance by those whose orders would be strict. Not only the troops of the Elector would watch it, but their own militia would guard this route between the two countries. Whichever group might see them, it was not in their interest for anyone at all to note their passing or to mention it abroad. It was best that no one know a group of Sisters of Silence now traveled toward the east.

That fact created a problem, for Lehnik had never heard of anyone ever crossing the Kell in the midst of the marsh. Those wide wastes of rushes and marsh flowers and treacherous stretches of bog-grass had been swallowing the three-horned deer and other native beasts for millennia. Whole herds of cattle brought by the colonists had disappeared into its bottomless maw.

Lehnik had no doubt that many a traveler, seeking to move in secret, must have also left his bones to soften and mix with those of the lost animals, as well. But no one had survived to spread any tale of the difficulty of his attempt.

The four Sisters stood quietly on the riverbank, letting their horses crop the lush grass while they looked thoughtfully across the channel toward the mazes of the marsh, showing every shade from yellow to blue-green in the misty sunlight. Where the grass was darkest green, the footing would be most treacherous, but in the full flush of spring almost everything was very green indeed. It was impossible to pick out any solid ridge of ground by the shade of its grass.

Benthe, standing beside Lehnik, murmured, half to himself, "Should we, then, go out and wade along the edge of the sea itself? Our mission is too important to risk losing everything in trying to cross there."

Lehnik sighed. "At Kell-mouth, so many small streams find their way to the sea that the currents are always boiling. Those eddies wash away the sand to a great depth, in places, and the sinkholes change constantly. It would be necessary to swim much of the way, and even horses find it very difficult to manage in the currents that exist there."

He fingered his jaw through the veil, thinking hard. "But we must cross. It cannot be by the road. I cannot think of an alternative."

Sister Sallek touched his sleeve. Her fingers busily spelled out, "There is another way to cross Kell-marsh. The denizens of the marsh have their own routes, which are possible for us and our horses."

Lehnik impatiently gestured, "But we don't know those ways and have no way of finding them."

Her small fingers moved again. "That is my talent, Sister Lehnik. I am able to link with small creatures, the native beings of this world that our ancestors called Halash."

He stared at her for a long moment. He had almost forgotten in the turmoil of his life as a soldier and the strain of becoming one of her Order that there were other sorts of creatures here, native to these lands. They had their roots in this world and knew its ways as none of his kind had ever managed to do.

Now he remembered that most of those native animals had been decimated or worse by the encroachment of Man upon their living spaces. The beasts and plants brought on the starships had changed many elements of this world, making certain parts of it uninhabitable for those who belonged here. Yet he had wondered if some might not exist, still, in remote and inhospitable crannies of the lands where no human advantage could be found.

"You *link*?" he asked aloud. He had never heard, even from rumor, that any of Halash's native beasts might be intelligent.

"There have always been a few who could relate to the Harveem and the Skerl," Sallek said, also aloud. Her voice was very soft. "We do not make our abilities known, for most of our kind here fear those beings as a threat or a danger. In that marsh live the

81

Harveem. They have their own system of roads, their fields and cities, although they are invisible to humankind." She cocked her head, her eyes above the veil assessing him closely.

Seeming reassured, she gazed toward the marsh. "Though our kind has endangered theirs incalculably, those people do not hold any bitterness toward us. They are very unlike human beings, for they accept things as they are, without anger. They will help us, I think, but you must wait here."

She gestured toward a clump of corund. "Hide there for a time, in the shade of the corund. I will try to make contact with the Harveem."

Lehnik nodded, his mind a turmoil of rearranged ideas. With the others, leading the horses, he withdrew into the bushes and peered out between the round planes of the leaves. Sallek dismounted, as he watched, and moved alone toward the rank growth that edged the River Kell.

CHAPTER TEN

Sallek stood as if she might be calling to someone or something, but no sound could be heard. He strained to catch the subdued flutter that troubled his thoughts, but he could grasp only a hint of the moth-wing signals with which he knew the Sister was calling to the Harveem.

In a short while another flutter joined the first, this one subtly alien, totally unfamiliar as it moved inside his skull. There were not even hints of words in that one, and Lehnik could not guess at the message. It had to be the reply of the Harveem.

Now the tide beyond Kell-mouth had turned. The wind whipped up from the sea, making the corund leaves flap wildly and sending Sallek's robe flapping about her small form. Blown sand and salt stung Lehnik's eyes and forehead until he pulled the veiling close, though he peered through the slit left open, still watching the Sister on the river bank.

She did not move. She looked as if she might be braced against some invisible barrier, bent forward with the intensity of her effort. She stood so for a long while before relaxing at last. Then she turned toward the thicket where her fellows waited.

Lehnik led the group out to meet her and found that she looked weary and subtly battered. But triumph shone in her gaze.

"They will aid us," she signaled. "We have but to cross the main stream to that low mound of grass just upstream." Lehnik followed her gesture, and he thought he could see a minimally higher roll of vegetation there.

"It's a pity there are no rocks here," he said aloud. "We could use the line-thrower that Speaker used to cross the Alt-Venn, if there were something to anchor to."

However, there was nothing solid on the other side to which any line might have been made fast. Almost all the area was either water or weed or swamp.

Benthe moved forward. "I have the strongest horse," he said. "Give me a line, and I will swim her across and anchor the cable to her saddle. Then the rest of you can come over with some support."

No one could think of a better plan, so Lehnik untied his own strong rope from the cantle of his saddle and handed one end to the sergeant. He fastened the other end to a scrubby corund that struggled for foothold at the water's edge, after testing to be sure that its roots were solidly set in the wet ground.

Benthe urged his stocky Janna into the stream, checking the depth frequently before moving her forward, bit by bit, into the current. Slowed by the turning tide, the current was not as strong as it had been before, and the stream was not extremely deep. Sand from the marshes and the banks had silted the river, making the slopes up and down the banks fairly gradual, as well.

Only when she reached the middle of the stream did Janna labor to keep from being swept toward the sea. She turned her square head slightly upstream, churning with her sturdy legs. Benthe slid along her back into the water and swam alongside, holding to the saddle-straps.

Relieved of his weight, she crossed with some effort into calmer water. Soon her hooves touched the bottom again, and Benthe ran beside her as she surged out of the water. They both rested for a time before he positioned her to hold the sustaining rope.

At last he signaled by twitching the rope. Lehnik was amused to find the sergeant was already adapting himself to the wordless life without seeming to think overmuch about it.

Sallek rode her black into the water, where the gelding snorted and danced. She sent him on, just upstream of the rope. When they came to the most difficult part of the current, she caught the rope and braced her side against it, holding the horse with her legs as it struggled forward and she pulled hand over hand.

That bit of help allowed the black to cross with much less difficulty than Janna had found. As the others followed, they found it easier yet. Lehnik, coming last, loosed the rope from the bush and had less stability, but he too found it possible to pass without difficulty.

As he drew near, Benthe coiled the rope around his saddle-tree. When they stood together on the other bank, safe and wet, Sallek faced toward the marsh once again. This time she called aloud, a fluting note followed by a trill.

As they waited, tense and expectant, a long gray head popped up from the water of the long slough that ran behind the river bank.

The head came toward them, pushing a slight bow-wave beneath its chin. Round yellow eyes examined them closely before blinking. Lehnik saw the eyelids were vertical, closing from the sides toward the upper part of the flat nose. A very strange creature indeed, he thought.

Benthe gestured toward the approaching animal and turned to Sallek with a question in every line of his body.

"Harveem," said Sallek, her voice almost too quiet to hear.

Lehnik was bursting with questions, too, but he managed to control them. All his life he had seen those sleek creatures gamboling in the waters of rivers and lakes, but he had never thought they might be sentient beings. Never had he even wondered about them.

A rapid pulsing against the walls of his mind told him the Harveem must be communicating with Sallek. Then it reached with a wet-furred gray arm to pull itself toward the hummock where they stood. When it waded out of the water, Lehnik could see it was shaped something like a very short, stumpy human being.

Its legs were shorter, its arms longer, and its entire body seemed very flexible. Though it had fur, there was no tail behind it. Now it was out of the water he could see that its ears had unclenched from its skull and become pointed sound-scoops. The nose, which had been flat, expanded too and became something like a human one.

The Harveem turned its gaze from Sallek to Lehnik and moved nearer. It offered a silver-gray paw and said, "Lay-neek."

Stunned, he took the paw into his hand, palm to palm in the sign of friendship and trust, evidently among this kind as it was among the Sisters. He had no way of knowing what it was Sallek said to it, but he tried to read the situation and the being before him as well as possible.

The creature turned now to the other two Sisters. Benthe and Kerrill went through the ritual of welcome, and while that took place Lehnik found his mind racing. A being with such rituals had to be intelligent.

In all the history of Halash there was only a single instance of a breach of trust after such a handclasp ritual. That tale was one used still to warn the young about the ultimate price of a lack of honor.

The Harveem stepped back to the edge of the water. It pointed a horn-tipped finger toward itself. "Har-looh," it said. "Will hellp across. Sallek tell...you will not betray to other man. Come!"

Without waiting to see if they followed, Har-looh moved into the shallow waters of the slough. Lehnik followed him, for there was nothing else to be done.

Sallek led her black into the sluggish whorls of mud and algae that followed the Harveem's route. Benthe went just behind her, leading Janna. After a glance at Lehnik, Kerrill took his gray after them, and Lehnik came last, wondering what strange adventure his group had found here.

Beneath the muddy surface of the slough's bottom, his foot found a firm ridge of soil. If he stepped to left or right his foot sank at once, but if he stuck to the narrow track behind Har-looh the footing was solid.

They crossed that slough and angled across another patch of uneasy ground. Beyond this one lay a bog, showing no indication that it might be passable. But their guide set off with total confidence, leaving them no choice but to sigh and continue to follow.

Secure footing lurked just beneath a few inches of muck, much to Lehnik's relief. However, he kept his attention focused on setting his feet exactly in the muddy spots left by those going before him.

The sun was setting, by now, amid a high layer of cloud, which gave promise of rain to come. Dark bars of mist marked the distant sky above the sea to the north. There a storm already raged. Just what they needed to speed their journey, Lehnik thought.

As he moved, darkness came. Frightening as it was to traverse the bog by daylight, at night it was enough to try the stoutest spirit.

Sallek's information came back to his mind. "They have their roads and fields, their cities...." One of their roads, he was sure, lay beneath his feet at that moment. Quite probably the pools they passed, covered with algae or lush growths of reeds, were their fields.

Yet he wondered about their cities. Here, where it was obvious to any eye that nothing rose above the level of the swamp, it was impossible to see any indication of buildings. Nothing dug beneath the swamp could help being inundated.

At that moment, Har-looh stepped up onto something that looked perfectly level, from where Lehnik stood. The Harveem continued to climb into a clump of bushes that turned, as Lehnik entered it, into a dusky, waist-high forest.

The Sister marveled at this flawless camouflage. Even in the midst of the greenery, he couldn't see anything unnatural, yet he felt he might be about to find himself at the door of one of the Harveem cities.

A sandstone doorway was revealed behind a thick clump of prickly growth, waist-high to Kerrill. As they approached it, another

Harveem appeared and took the reins of their horses, leading them away into the deepening night.

Har-looh motioned for them to stoop and enter the door. Lehnik could find no alternative other than sitting all night in the swamp, waiting for the storm to wash him off the spit of land into the river.

Sallek entered the doorway first. The others followed her reluctantly, only to stop inside and marvel at a scene that would be a tale to tell about the fires in their dotage. A city lay before them. As they descended the shallow steps, Lehnik wondered that such a huge space could be kept dry, beneath such a marshy surface as that which lay above it. But the stairway and the cross corridors that appeared as they went were cut, it seemed, from solid stone, with no crevice left to admit moisture.

He found it hard to believe the sandy swamp above was underlaid by such a stony foundation. He had a sobering thought. Had the Harveem, sensing future danger at the hands of the newly arrived men, engineered the river in order to create that concealing marsh?

Knowing something of geology from his schooling, Lehnik found himself doubting that such a subsurface layer could possibly be entirely without flaw or fault. He watched closely as they followed Sallek, but he found no mark of chisel and no hint of a seam. His careful, accurate mind found it puzzling, and he was still thinking about the problem when he found himself facing a dozen of the gray-furred people.

Something pulsed inside his mind, touching his thought, but Lehnik had begun to recognize the fact that he had no talent whatsoever for mental communication. Evidently the Harveem came to the same conclusion, for the sleekest of them fixed a yellow gaze upon his face.

"Not forr long has yourrr kind stood herre!" it said. The tone was not entirely cordial, though it didn't quite seem hostile.

Sallek stepped forward. "Only in direst need would I have called upon you, Hrre-fell. Those Sisters who know you have done our best to keep your existence secret from the rest of our kind here on this world."

The round eyes narrowed to slits. The ears flattened against the curved skull. Lehnik understood that to one who could read the physical signals of the Harveem these changes might mean more than words were capable of carrying.

He watched closely as the creature replied. To his astonishment, it did not speak as men do, with tongue and lips and teeth. The sound was produced in some mysterious manner that involved the filling and emptying of some sort of space in the Harveem's upper shoulders. The result issued from its mouth, sounding as if produced by something like a bagpipe.

He was studying the method of speech so closely that he missed the words that were spoken. When he looked up into the creature's eyes, he found them filled with amusement.

"No, we do not speak as you do, but with thought-link we learned how mankind communicates. We learrned worrds and tones frrom the Sisterrs, overr many generrations. Now Harrveem can speak with men.

"Seldom do we choose to do that, forr the furr of our kind is sprread over many shoulderrs and couches of men, in yourr land and in Garrouche." The wry tone could not have been bettered by Speaker herself.

Lehnik found himself wondering how he would feel if he had found the walls of the Harveem city tapestried with the hides of humankind. The thought made him shudder.

Hrre-fell turned again to Sallek. "Therre is much trrouble, even herre. On the edge of the swamp there arre men who hide. They prrey upon anything they can eat. Unforrtunately, we arre only meat to them. They have brrought the warr in yourr lands to us. What might so few of you do to ease ourr losses?"

Sallek lifted her veil and let it fall about her shoulders. This revealed a small round face highlighted by a pug nose and determined gray eyes. She frowned as she spoke.

"There are weapons now in Garrouche that may put an end to life altogether, on this entire world. For you and for us and for everything else. Even the dangers you face here are better, I think." She sighed and picked at her veil with thin, nervous fingers.

"We have hinted to your kind, in the past, that our ancestors brought to this world things too perilous for use. Those were trusted to our keeping in the Houses of Silence. Now the Elector has broken the integrity of our house in Garrouche, and he has stolen the weapons guarded there."

The Harveem gave a strange sound, something between a hoot and a hiss.

But Sallek was continuing. "With those weapons he can make of this rich land a place where even serpents and insects will be unable to live. We are sent to remove those things from the hands of this one who would misuse them."

The creature's eyelids flicked open and shut and open again. Hrre-fell's stance relaxed from its former tension. Those standing beside their leader also seemed to unbend, though Lehnik under-stood that to be more a mental than a physical matter.

"Then be welcome in ourr place," said Hrre-fell. "Rrest and take food. It is no easy task you must accomplish...." The bagpipe voice trailed off, its tone thoughtful, and Lehnik wondered if the Harveem were reading details of their assignment directly from Sallek's mind.

He decided that such must have been the case, for no questions were asked by their hosts. No word was said about routes to be fol-lowed or methods to be used. Only food came forth, strange, green-tasting, but palatable.

Then they were led to couches of dried rushes. In his exhaus-tion, Lehnik found his more comfortable than the finest linen-hung bed he had ever occupied.

CHAPTER ELEVEN

Lehnik slept more deeply than he had done in many years. It was as if the rock-walled room in the depths of the Harveem city had provided such security that he could now allow his internal watchman to relax. That deeply buried guardian had been on duty since he was fifteen and had found his parents lying dead and mutilated amid the ruins of their business, after a raid.

The rest he found on this night seemed to remove from his body more than a decade of tension and wariness. He didn't even dream. Yet when he woke it was with the feeling that he had spoken with someone in those last few moments before waking.

Benthe had already risen and was washing in a curiously shaped basin. He turned, when Lehnik stirred, drying his hands on a bit of rough-woven cloth.

"Sallek has already been talking with the Harveem leaders," he said, his tone soft, as if he hated to speak, even here in privacy. "I'm relieved not to have to explain just what we're doing to those people. I don't more than half understand it myself."

Lehnik rose and took his place at the basin, pouring fresh water from a bowl on the small table. After he was done, he sat on the edge of the table and stared at the sergeant.

"I've been worrying whether the Harveem might decide just to let all the humans kill each other off, then take their own chances with whatever it is those weapons can do," he said. "I think they understood just what Sallek was saying when she described their effects, but I still felt odd. Now I feel no unease."

Benthe nodded, as if he had the same feeling.

It was obvious the Harveem had decided to help the Sisters as much as they were able. A dozen spokesmen joined the group in the chamber where food waited for them. Hrre-fell dipped a horny finger into a pot of something purple that he suspended from a cord at his side. With his stained finger, he drew on a slab of pale stone.

"Herre is the River Kell, as you call it, though we name it the Hhruuflomm. On the other side lies the land claimed by yourr countrry. Two days' jourrney, it coverrs. When you are clearr of the bog, therre is Garrouche." He dotted in an emphatic purple splotch.

"Far down here is the Elektorr's place. That is a long distance, and it is dangerrous, as things arre now. Dangerrous both forr yourr kind and forr mine. But therre are otherr ways than those yourr people know. You will need a Skerrl." Hrre-fell glanced toward Sallek. "You link with those, also?"

The small Sister nodded. Kerrill, beside her, seemed unsurprised, though Benthe's small brown eyes were wells of astonished wonder. Lehnik did not doubt his own expression was as puzzled as the sergeant's, for both knew the Skerl as small, four-legged animals with spiky fur that smelled of earth and roots.

Some people kept them as pets. This was not unusual, yet Sallek was indicating the Sisters mind-linked with the Skerl, and the idea seemed unthinkable. He realized, even as he had the thought, that it had seemed just as impossible for the Harveem to be intelligent beings with an entire culture undreamed-of by his kind.

Hrre-fell was continuing. "The Skerrl trravel the lands as they will, forr none see them as a thrreat. Ourr kind cannot go farr frrom the waterr, for we must have the wet soil, the mud, to keep ourrselves healthy. The landbound Skerrl, strrange as it may seem to you, seek us out when they have need. As we seek them."

So these two intelligent species (how many more might there be here, unsuspected and unnoted? Lehnik wondered) cooperated to solve common needs. Lehnik concentrated on the Harveem's next words.

"They know all lands, all rroads and trracks and paths used by the beasts alone. They know ways that arre marrked by none, yet which arre passable. Theirr ways are hidden and forr that rreason they will be much less dangerrous for you to trravel. You have need of at least one Skerrl. Yet we cannot call to them until you arre clearr of our barrierrs."

Lehnik stared at Hrre-fell sharply. The Harveem gave its version of a smile.

"You think truly," it said. "We set the waterrways, melted and rreset the stone, engineerred this swamp as a rretrreat into which yourr kind would neverr come without drriving need. Ourr farr ancestorrs shaped this place forr us. The weapons they possessed, such as they arre, have not been lost to us."

Lehnik did not miss the sarcasm hidden not too deeply in the creature's words. As he glanced aside at Benthe, a slender Harveem entered the room and touched the leader's furry shoulder.

Hrre-fell nodded. "Yourr mounts are past the dangerr point now. It is time forr you to join them."

After stepping through the sandstone doorway and out of the low clump of bushes, Lehnik turned to look back. If his existence had depended upon his finding it again, he would have been lost, for the entry to the Harveem town was dissolved into the swamp, invisible to any but the most knowing eye.

He sighed, his attention now needed for setting his feet exactly into the track of the Sister just ahead of him. Here the quagmire was forbidding. The road was more like a path of single stone flags, all covered with mud and water.

The wind, now mixed with pellets of rain, was also distracting. It rippled the thick waters, erasing the disturbed silt that marked the spot where the preceding foot had stepped last. He had to use all his wit and skill to stay on the path.

The bushes, which were an integral part of the swamp ecology, were pushed southward by the sea winds, their position so unwavering that he thought at first they grew that way. Only when the flat gale eased at last did they begin bobbing about. No one could possibly memorize the shapes of individual bushes in order to find the city of the Harveem again.

Not that he cared to do it. At that point he felt water trickling from collar to heel, despite his sturdy white robe with its attached hood. His feet were soaked, feeling puffy and tender, and his eyes stung with wind-borne salt.

It was a relief when the Harveem guide paused. Lehnik felt soil beneath his sodden boots. Wet and soft, it was not swamp but honest dirt.

His companions looked as bedraggled as he felt. All turned toward their mounts, which were held by a pair of furry shapes. Lehnik felt more enthusiasm than he would have felt possible, for even weary hours in the saddle seemed better than this blind trek through a morass.

No one spoke, for the intensity of the gale would have thrust any words back into the teeth of a speaker. Instead, Lehnik repeated the hand ritual, and his fellows followed suit.

The Harveem responded and turned to slide into the waters through which the group had just come. Instantly, they were invisible.

Sallek set her foot into her high stirrup and vaulted into her saddle. "Skerl," she signed. "After we find shelter. They will not come out into such weather."

Lehnik nodded, his opinion of the good sense of the Skerl rising. Nothing intelligent would come out into weather like this unless driven by some mortal need.

They turned the heads of their mounts away from the wind and set out eastward across the grassy plain. In this area beyond the river, it was beginning to rise into low ridges and rolls, and small thickets of corund and berrybush grew on the lee sides of any hillock or clump of sheltering trees.

Even so far inland, Lehnik could see boulders that had obviously been carried from the coast by the fierce, wind-driven surges caused by the storms that racked this area. The stone matched that along the shoreline, and he shuddered to think of the force that had brought them so far.

Lehnik's horse was more than glad to set his back to the gale, and he moved quickly through the pounding rain. At last, Lehnik realized they were reaching higher ground, for about them rose real hills, not hillocks or grassy dunes. Small garoaks found rooting space here, and arms of a scrubby forest thrust out in the direction in which they traveled.

When the hills closed about them, their cloak of woods sheltering the travelers from the blast, Sallek pulled into the thickest spinney she could find. She motioned for Lehnik to come near.

Once out of the worst of the wind, it was again possible to hear, and she spoke aloud for brevity's sake. "We can stop in the lee of that big hill ahead."

Lehnik, squinting, made out a considerable height off to their left and nodded.

"The Skerl will come, even in this, now that we are out of the unsheltered ways. I must be perfectly quiet and focused in order to send my call. Yet we will make up the loss of time because of our increased speed. The Skerl will guide us by the shortest and safest route."

Again he nodded. It was strange how reluctant he was, now, to rely on the spoken word. He had not realized before how calm and balanced his mind had become during its time of total silence.

Behind the hill it was relatively quiet. The Sisters backed the horses into a thicket of small garoaks and huddled beside them, glad of this protection from the weather. Sallek handed her reins to

Lehnik and stood, eyes closed and effort beginning to show in the lines of her body.

For an instant, Lehnik thought he felt a trace of her call wisping against his mind. Then it was gone, and he was left with wet leaves slapping against his cloak.

The sky was dark with cloud and rain, the sort of weather he had endured many times in his military career. He hardly noticed his discomfort but remained alert, his eyes noting anything unusual, his ears cocked for any sound that was not wind in leaves.

They were now in enemy territory. Although still technically inside the boundaries of Trans-Kell, he was certain this country was now in the hands of unfriendly forces.

Something caught his eye, a motion, a flash of white at the edge of a thicket on the side of the hill beyond the cupped valley to the lee of his shelter. He turned his head slowly, carefully, so as to avoid moving leaves against the wind or otherwise betraying his position.

There were three shapes there, now, small blurs but easily detected. He reached behind him to touch Benthe and twitched at his sleeve to get his attention. Even as he pointed, those three shapes moved out of the thicket's shelter into the wind, moving toward the hill under which they huddled.

Benthe hissed between his teeth. A horse stamped, squishing its hoof in the mud as Kerrill appeared beside Lehnik.

The tall Sister's hands moved before Lehnik's eyes. "No danger," they signaled. "Sisters approach."

Sisters? Lehnik found himself wondering who might be abroad in such a storm and in enemy-held territory. Could these possibly be the three whom the horse dealer had watched cross the Kell, so many days before?

If so, why were they again on this side of the river? Why had they not gone directly to Chelos? Or could these be fugitives from the breached House of Garrouche?

Now the trio were on the wind-whipped grass, moving on foot, leading one horse, which was lame. They struggled forward, the wind-driven rain lashing about their bodies, and as they drew nearer Lehnik saw that one of the Sisters was limping painfully.

He glanced toward Sallek, but she was still, eyes closed, totally concentrated upon her task of calling the Skerl. He looked up at Kerrill, who nodded. They tied the reins they held to a sapling and started across the wet grass toward the newcomers.

Those three seemed unsurprised to see their own kind coming to help them. Lehnik thought they had been drawn from cover by the same call Sallek was sending to the Skerl. His own inability to take part in such mental communication was beginning to trouble him.

Then he pushed aside the thought as he set an arm about the limping Sister and helped her toward the shelter of the thicket. No words were needed. He felt her relief when they reached the others and he could allow her to lean against a tree while he helped her companions into the spinney.

The lame animal could carry much of the burden their pack horse had borne, so they offloaded that and distributed any extra among the mounted Sisters. This left three riders for two mounts.

This problem was solved when the smallest of the three pointed toward Sallek, then at herself. Two such lightweights should not overburden the sturdy black pack horse, it was obvious.

When Sallek opened her eyes, she found three new companions with her group, but she seemed quite unsurprised. At once she agreed to riding double. Then she motioned toward the south and mounted, pulling the new Sister up behind her.

Lehnik sighed. It seemed the Skerl had agreed to meet them, though he'd had his doubts. He mounted his roan and followed the little troop away from the thicket, into the rain. But something inside nagged at him. There were enemies here, and at no great distance, or his instincts had betrayed him.

There was no time and there were insufficient numbers to investigate the countryside. He could only go forward to meet the Skerl. That and whatever else this miserable day might hold in store for this bedraggled group of Sisters.

CHAPTER TWELVE

As the riders worked their way deeper into the hills, the storm settled into a steady rain, the wind dying bit by bit to gusts and then to quiet. Spring though it might be, Lehnik found himself chilled to his bones, and even his horse shivered between his knees.

He had no doubt his companions were also cold, though of course nothing was said. He heard someone beginning to wheeze as she breathed, and his own lungs felt as if he were breathing under water. Indeed, harsh breathing turned into coughs as the small troop rode through the downpour.

They followed no visible track. Sallek led them as she homed on her contact with the Skerl. As they followed her sensing, the long day of riding passed with infrequent rests and no shelter that was more water repellent than an occasional corund. Even then, the plate-shaped leaves were as likely to dump a gallon of water down your neck as to protect you from the wet.

Even the horses seemed unwilling to pause in the constant rainfall, so the Sisters walked and led them when they tired. Wet feet slogged through mud and soggy mulch of dead leaves, as well as puddled water in stump holes.

When Sallek stopped at last it was almost nightfall. Her hand moved, and Lehnik hoped to the bottom of his heart the signal meant they were near the Skerl.

It did. From the dripping undergrowth there emerged a small creature exactly the shade of the wet, dead leaves. It moved toward them like a streak, pausing just before it ran under Sallek's horse. When it rose onto its hind feet, Lehnik could see that those were flat and square, with ankle-like joints that made it possible for the creature to stand erect.

Silent signals moved between Sister and Skerl. Lehnik could detect nothing, though the other Sisters, except for Benthe, seemed to know what was happening. All three of the newcomers nodded vigorously, as did Kerrill. Lehnik stood beside Benthe, whose head was bent as he endured this strangest of duties with the resignation of an old soldier.

The communication did not take long. Sallek turned toward her companions and gestured them forward and to the right. Now they mounted again, the Skerl skittering before them through the low growth. It led them around a hill, through a thick copse of the largest trees they had seen this side of the river. There they emerged onto a well traveled clay road.

Lehnik urged his mount forward, coming level with Sallek's. He reached to tug at her sleeve. Then, pointing down the road, he raised his eyebrows in an unspoken question.

The small Sister said aloud, "The Skerl indicates that no one is on this road for a very long distance. Nor has there been any traveler along it for days. There is a good inn where the road curves to meet the small ford over the Kell, and we think it best for our group to sleep dry and warm tonight." She smiled at his expression.

"Our mission will not offer many such chances. And if we become ill, it may hinder our speed and our purpose far more than this small delay. Some are already coughing." She didn't look at him directly, but Lehnik knew she could hear his own chest beginning to bubble and wheeze.

She was staring at the injured Sister, who now rode behind Benthe and obviously held herself on the horse by will alone, joined to her desperate grip about the sergeant's waist. Even as Lehnik watched, she wavered and almost fell.

He knew this made sense. With a change to dry clothing, a hot-tubbing, and beds worthy of the name, they might find themselves far more capable of going ahead tomorrow. If they should camp outdoors in the wet, without a fire and subject to the damp chill, it would be evil for them all. The rain had now slowed to a drizzle, but the ground was soaked, and no one could hope to sleep dry in the forest tonight.

As if sensing that food and shelter lay ahead, the horses picked up their weary hooves and clattered among the gravels of the road to make good speed. Before it was fully dark, the warm lights of the inn shone through the trees, cheering everyone mightily.

They rode at last into a stone-flagged courtyard, whose walls enclosed large stables and the entry porch of the capacious inn. A scraggly boy ran out into the wet and began taking the reins from their chilled fingers.

The innkeeper himself appeared in the doorway to greet them. His rotund figure spoke well for the cookery in his establishment as he came forward to direct still another boy to take their packs into the inn. With his own hands, he lifted down the wounded Sister from her horse and supported her into the hall.

He led them all into a comfortable sitting room, where a fire roared hugely in the stone hearth. He deposited the Sister in a chair near the blaze and turned to the rest.

"There will be someone to take you to your rooms in a moment," he bumbled. "I will have Tallia set the stew back on the fire... she outdid herself tonight, and only the fact that so few travel the roads these days allow any to be left at all. Now come and dry yourselves. Get warm! The rooms will be ready at once!"

They accepted his invitation, gathering around the hearth to hear their own damp begin to sizzle and steam from their clothing. Soon the smell of wet cloth and horses and mud filled the room.

That didn't bother any of them, though they were happy when a skinny girl came to the door and squeaked, "Rooms be done. Three to one, four to t'other."

They found their chambers to be clean, low-ceiled, and sparsely furnished. Pallets, simple but clean and soft, and stools formed the fittings, and pegs screwed into the walls held their clothing. Soon Lehnik, Benthe, and Kerrill were stripped to the waist, washing at the bench where ewers of hot water steamed gently.

As Lehnik pulled on dry clothing from his oilskin pack and donned dry slippers, he mused on what a great difference small comforts can make in a person's outlook. He felt almost cheerful as he followed his freshly white-robed and veiled companions into the hallway.

There their fellows from the room across the hall met them. All went down together, Sallek helping the injured Sister, who seemed both ill and exhausted. She resisted the notion of having food sent up to the room, however, and they humored her desire to remain with the rest.

The stew was everything the innkeeper promised. Lehnik could almost feel his strength pouring back into him, and the discomfort in his chest subsided when the innkeeper urged upon him a cup of healing tea. Across the table, he could see the small Sister straighten. Above her veil, her black eyes sparked with new energy, and that promised well for their plans for tomorrow.

Hot mint tea and rich bread and cheese filled every available chink in Lehnik's belly, and by the time the meal was done he felt ready for anything. But hardly had they completed their meal when there was a clatter of hooves in the courtyard.

Rough voices called harshly for the stable boy and the inn-keeper. Not wishing to meet any of the troopers of Garrouche, the seven rose from their places to return to their rooms. Before they could leave, however, a group of men stamped in at the door.

Those were heavily armed, and they did not offer to lay aside their weapons, as was the custom when one entered an inn. Their faces were dirty, some bearded, all forbidding. They were obviously not troopers, whatever else they might be.

"So, there be company tonight, eh?" growled the leader, who was far older than the rest. "And female company, at that." He stared rudely at the white-clad Sisters, his thought plain in his eyes.

"Ye cannot get luckier than that, say I. Come here, little-un," he said to Sallek, who was passing him to reach the stair. "I like a woman to keep a still tongue. Saves a muckle of gab and time."

She eluded his awkward grab with ease and was halfway up the flight of steps before he was fully aware that he had missed catching her. The other six were following her closely, turning their backs on the hubbub of cursing and commands and general bedlam that the newcomers brought into the inn.

When they reached the top of the stair, they found the skinny girl close behind them. An older woman came, too, her stringy hair straggling from beneath her cap. "Fayven sent us up," she said.

"He doesn't hold with such trash as that below, but he has no power to turn 'em away. He says you must lock your doors and wedge them wi' the stools tonight. Those toughs have been here afore this, and always they make trouble for any that are here."

The injured Sister motioned for them all to come into the room shared by the female Sisters. They did so and closed the door behind them, barring it then and wedging it fast. She sat suddenly on a spare stool, gripping her hurt leg tightly, as if to control considerable pain. When she looked up she spoke aloud, but very quietly.

"I think those may be the very rogues who ambushed us at the small ford yesterday. We were driven back across the Kell, after crossing days earlier, by movements of troops. We were attempting to cross again at this minor ford when, without warning or demands of any kind, they sent a flight of arrows out of the bushes. Two of our mounts were killed.

"We all went into the deep pool downstream from the ford, instead of trying for either bank. We came ashore around the bend and had time to meet them with steel when they came looking for us.

99

There were only a few there, at that time, and not one of them returned to report what had happened to the rest. Yet we lost our mounts, and I had an arrow in my leg.

"We decided to take cover in the forest and wait for the chance to cross again. As the ford was closed to us, we kept moving northward as fast as we could manage, for we wanted to try the bridge near Kell-mouth. And so we found you, in the end."

Lehnik looked down at her with concern. "Are you from the House of Silence in Trans-Kell? Are you, in fact, the three who bore word of the invasion toward Chelos, many days ago?"

She shook her head. "We are from the House of Garrouche. After completing a mission for the Elector, we returned home, only to find it in the hands of those with no right there. That is when we turned toward Trans-Kell, knowing your strong mountain location to be all but impregnable."

"There has been no move against our House," said Lehnik. "We are on a mission, and although I am only half trained as a Sister and lack much knowledge, I was assigned to lead this expedition." He turned to Kerrill, who nodded.

"Any Sister can hear any secret," the big Sister said. "No others can possibly endure the training or the silence or the necessity for living inside themselves in peace. We may tell these Sisters about our task, Sister Lehnik. It may be that they, being from Garrouche, can help us achieve our goal."

His words made good sense. Feeling reassured, Lehnik said, "Then I will go to my bed and allow you to convey the information between minds. Although I feel better now, I almost became ill today, in the wet and the chill, and it will not come amiss to rest."

He crossed the hall and entered the other room, but he did not fasten his door tightly, for he knew that Benthe and Kerrill would soon be coming. His pallet was thick, keeping away from his bones the chill of the floor, and the coverings were warm.

Lehnik tucked his robe and veil closely about him and lay down, pulling the covers about his neck. He fell into a deep and rather feverish slumber.

Something, not the soft movements of one of the Order as he prepared for sleep, roused him after some time. A clumsy step, the whisper of a drunken curse, brought him completely awake. He lay motionless, trying to determine what was happening.

"Jus' one c'm out'n went in here. All by her little lonesome!" There was a muffled laugh. Then the door burst inward, and two men threw themselves across Lehnik, as he rose from his pallet.

100

Never in his life of rough living among the militia had he expected someone might try to rape him. He found himself filled with fury as he came up, tumbling them aside, and prepared for battle.

There was a grunt at the door. Lehnik could see from the corner of his eye that Benthe stood there, his stocky shape unmistakable, even in its whites. He was obviously assessing the situation, but before he could make up his mind, one of those wrestling with Lehnik sprang up and tackled this other "Sister."

"Got one o' m'own!" he shouted, catching the burly sergeant about the waist. "Flat as a slab!" was his next remark, which seemed tinged with disappointment. "They mus' jus' take th' hopeless 'uns."

Engaged as he was in trying to keep his own attacker's hands away from his person, Lehnik found himself chuckling at what had to be going on inside Benthe's head. Not only had these idiots mistaken him for a proper subject for rape, they had also found him disappointing. That had to be doubly infuriating.

Lehnik found himself laughing as the evil-smelling drunkard atop him rolled and tussled and tried to rip the tough robe and veil from his body. More feet pounded on the stair, while he struggled.

"They're at the women!" came a shout.

Lehnik gave a precisely gauged heave, tossing his assailant against the wall. The man's head cracked against the painted wood, and he slid down to sit on the floor, his eyes cocked in different directions.

Four more raiders tried to crowd in at once, plugging the opening with their struggling bodies for a moment. While they were trying to untangle themselves, Benthe caught his would-be amour around the neck with both hands. He lifted the man off his feet, his legs kicking wildly.

The wily sergeant had learned all the tricks of hand-to-hand combat before the young tough between his hands had been weaned, and he shook the stripling roughly, almost throttling him. Then he flung him sideways, into the pair who had at last managed to get inside the door.

They all went backward against the wall, dazed and disorganized. Lehnik now had his blade in hand. Benthe leaped, turning in mid-air, to come down standing beside him. His own shortsword appeared in his white-gloved hand.

The befuddled four at the wall stood, mouths open, trying to make sense of this unexpected turnabout. Their drunken minds were slowly realizing that rapes were not supposed to proceed this way.

101

More feet clattered on the stair as the last trio of raiders, led by their chief, burst into the room. "Save one for me!" the older man was yelling. Then he saw the situation and stopped suddenly.

Not even the most ignorant and drunken mercenary was fool enough to attack a Sister of Silence who was armed and waiting for him. Here were two, though they faced more than three times their number. Enough rationality was left in the old man to make him pause to consider.

Before he could decide what to do, there came a quiet stir behind him in the hallway. Lehnik saw the glint of a long knife as it came from behind to lie across the raider's throat.

With some amusement, he saw his white-robed fellows come into the room, gently nudging the drunken crew with their knives until all were in line, facing the wall against which their unconscious brother was lying. They seemed stunned at the sudden reversal.

Lehnik wondered, in his turn, what might be best to do. It was against his new training, as well as his personal inclinations, to kill helpless men. Yet he could only feel that to let them run free again, preying on the farms and settlements, would be far worse.

Benthe tugged at his sleeve, drawing him from the room. Once they were in the hall, the sergeant leaned toward him. "We should tie 'em up, tight as can be, and in the morning we can turn 'em over to the innkeeper. I've a notion these men have much to answer for, 'round about here.

"I'll be no end surprised if there is not a great hanging in the next day or so. With dancing and singing and general rejoicing, or I miss my guess. What do you think of my plan?"

Lehnik grinned behind his veil. Good old Benthe. Always there with common sense.

"Just right," he said. "Now let's tie these villains and stack them like cordwood in the hall for the night. I'm ready for my rest, and I don't doubt the others are, too. I've an idea our host will be more than pleased to have the disposal of these beasts. His wife, too...she looked terrified."

They returned to the bedchamber to begin roping their captives. Lehnik found himself chuckling from time to time at the thought of Benthe's shock at his predicament.

He felt much better. The fever seemed to be gone. Again, he felt well and ready for anything that might come his way.

CHAPTER THIRTEEN

One short year before, the swordplay, the confrontation with villains, and the excitement of the evening would have left Lehnik unable to sleep. He would have lain awake, reliving the episode, re-thinking his tactics, for hours. But the time in the House of Silence had taught him control. The moment he closed his eyes, he released all thoughts of the past and fell asleep at once.

A step in the corridor, cautious and mouse-like, woke him just after dawn. Light showed at the narrow-paned window, though the sun was not yet up. The sky looked almost clear through the grimy panes.

He sat, smoothly and noiselessly, and rose to tiptoe to the door. He knew before he opened the panel that the innkeeper stood out-side. He joined Fayven, who was staring down at the untidy bundles that were his other guests.

"How would you like to have the disposal of these villains?" he asked. "We have no time and no authority here to try and hang ban-dits."

Fayven glanced along the untidy row of unconscious men. "They are all alive?" he quavered.

"Of course. One has a large bump on his head and the others sport various cuts and bruises, but we thought it best to let you, who know who has suffered most at their hands, take charge and help to decide their fate. We dislike bloodshed, though it seems that we may indulge in quite a bit more before we are done."

The round face lifted to his. In the gloom of the hall he could see Fayven's mouth widen into a grin that promised no good for the bandits.

"There is nothing that we hereabout would like more than a chance to mark *paid* to this crew. They have pilfered and raided and raped among us for a good month now. Before that I think they plied their trade farther to the east, but were run out by the troops moving about."

His grin turned wicked. "You may be sure, we'll give 'em nothing but the justice they've earned."

Lehnik nodded. "Then roust out Tallia and ask if she will make us a big breakfast. We must be on our way almost at once." Behind him in their room, Lehnik could hear stirring as his two companions rose and washed.

Fayven grunted. "She rose before day. Already she has new bread in the ovens, for it rose overnight. I have been saving a deer haunch that is aged just right for eating. You will sit down to a meal that cannot be bettered, even in Chelos itself," he boasted.

* * * * * * *

They rode out in the first sunlight, and Lehnik found himself agreeing with Fayven's assessment of their meal. The excellence of the fare and the smiles on the faces of the family at the inn told him much about the fears such bandit raiders must be rousing in the people along the Kell.

It was evident from what Fayven said that there had been unrest in Garrouche long before the invasion of Trans-Kell ever began. Possibly, the Elector had decided to send hand-picked bands of "criminals" across the border in order to harry the nearby inhabitants of his neighboring country, softening it up for his major thrust.

Sallek reined in her mount to allow him to catch up to her. She had been following the unobtrusive shape of the Skerl, which now turned off the road onto a dim track that led into forested hills. Now they were well away from the coast, the woods were becoming darker, the trees larger and their branches thicker overhead.

He paused and allowed the rest to pass him. Then, last of all, he heeled his chestnut into the almost invisible track, reined him in, and dismounted. A branch of dead leaves, broken in some autumn storm, lay beside the trail, and he caught it up and used it to sweep away the faint prints of hooves that had ruffled the layers of dead leaves over which the beasts passed.

It was impossible to remove all traces of disturbance, but he smoothed the way well enough so that no one who didn't search specifically for their trail would notice it as they passed on the road. When he caught up with the others, they had dismounted to wait for him.

Sallek pointed ahead, and Lehnik followed her gesture with his gaze. The Skerl waited, too, close against what seemed to be an impenetrable hedge; there seemed to be no place to pass in the spot where he stood. Yet it was plain the creature wanted them to follow it.

Lehnik led the chestnut and the packhorse and strode toward the thick wall of greenery. The little creature gave a soft sound, half growl and half purr, before ducking into a gap that had been invisible before, even at point-blank range.

Lehnik ducked as low as possible without going onto all-fours and followed. The horses shouldered aside the branches and came after him. When he turned, the branches had sprung back into place, leaving, as far as he could see, no trace of having been moved at all.

Once past that point, he stayed busy keeping the Skerl in sight. He followed through a maze of bushes, trees, and boulders. Behind them, he could hear the slight sounds of movement as his companions and their mounts came along in his wake. As the morning wore on, it became entirely too warm, there beneath the thick canopy of branches, but the Skerl did not pause and neither did his followers.

Only when they emerged into a clearing at the top of a hill did the procession halt. Lehnik looked toward the south to find it was past mid-day. The wooded hills were glowing with spring, green and ocher buds glowing in the sunlight, and far down in the valley below he could see the sparkle that marked a curve in the course of the Kell. Off to the west a long vale gave a glimpse of one of the hill towns that clung to the steeps above the river.

Something about the terrain seemed subtly wrong, and Lehnik motioned to Benthe. The sergeant took out his long glass and adjusted it before peering east, west, and south. He handed it to Lehnik at last, his face grim.

When Lehnik trained the glass on the town he had seen, he found it had been burned. There was no sign of life there, except a smudge of smoke rising in a thin column. The white stone of the houses was blackened by fire. Most of the buildings were roofless.

Bile rose in his throat, as he thought of the friendly, hard-working people he had known in that tiny hamlet. Why should the Elector take upon himself the right to bring grief to people who had never harmed him?

The wounded Sister tugged at his arm. "There!" she said, pointing southeastward. "That is where the Kell curves sharply to the east, where the ford is, and we must avoid that area. Because of a long stretch of rapids that keeps anyone from crossing for miles on either side, all roads join there. To avoid going many miles out of our way, we must cross the main road. The Skerl will lead us along secret ways, and we must be across before nightfall tomorrow."

Even as Lehnik stared at the thread marking the main road, there came a flicker of motion there. The long-glass revealed a column of mounted troops, moving along at a good rate. Lehnik recalled the course of the road, which led from Kell-Ford at an amble toward the northeast border where Garrouche met Trans-Kell. There was a permanent military post there on the other side.

He found himself wondering if any of the men he had known survived there. He had served with several of those permanently assigned to the watch point.

Then there was no time for musing. If he could see the column with his glass, then someone in that distant group, deciding to survey the surrounding hills through his own, might well glimpse the white-clad group at the edge of the trees.

He motioned for the Sisters to reenter the forest, and they moved at once. He felt better when all were under cover again. In the dappled shadows of the wood, their robes were less of a liability, but they would be visible from a great distance once the Sisters went out into the sunlight.

Kerrill, at his elbow, was following his thoughts. "We should roll in the wood loam, I think," he gestured. "We are too visible, and even the blue linings of our robes would not disappear against so much greenery. As couriers, we must be highly visible. On this mission it is not good to be visible at all."

Lehnik grunted agreement, and Benthe exhaled a long sigh of relief. "I've been wonderin' if we must walk into the Stronghold, all white and tidy. Seemed less than wise to me, though I trust the Sisters. Now I trust 'em even more."

Lehnik raised his head above the bush behind which they had retired and surveyed the terrain just ahead. A huge garoak had blown down in some bygone storm, leaving a cup of soil and dead leaves. There the roots had pulled away, and in the loose soil about them Benthe proceeded to roll himself heartily.

When he rose, he shook himself. "How is it now?" Benthe asked, turning around so his companions could examine all sides.

It was excellent camouflage, and Lehnik took his turn, as did the others. When they set out, they formed as grimy a group as he had ever seen, blending well into the forest.

Now the Skerl led them down unexpected layers of shallow cliffs. They crossed gravel beds at the edges of creeks leading from their sources as springs in the hills to lose themselves in the Kell. The group saw no road or path formed by the goings and comings of mankind. Even game trails were infrequent.

106

No normal traveler would ever have dreamed of choosing the routes they took. Only wild native creatures, shrewd and knowledgeable as the Skerl, could have understood or used those ways.

The going was not easy, and they walked most of the time, leading their mounts. Sallek let Lehnik lead her horse, for she was occupied with keeping her thought attuned to the Skerl, though it was now easier to keep the linkage than before.

She could crawl after it, for she was small, into crannies that would have been difficult for Lehnik to fit into. Once the way was located, of course, the others managed to open them out to fit the larger Sisters, concealing all sign of their passing as the last came through. One of their number always remained behind to lead the horses around the obstacles, brushing away all trace of their passing.

Night found them camped in a hollow among tremendous trees. Just beyond a small ridge, a spring trickled into a stone basin, and they watered their horses there, after filling their water bottles. They never considered camping near the water. Lehnik led them well out of sight, for anyone else moving through the country would also hunt out water and would tend to camp beside it.

All of them were weary. Even the tough sinews of the Sisters and the sergeant had been tried to their utmost, and Lehnik wondered how the wounded Sister managed to keep up with the rest. He noted over supper that she ate with determination rather than appetite and lay down at once in her chosen bed among tall ferns.

He crouched beside Sallek, who was mending one of her boots with thongs from her pack. "How badly is she hurt?" he asked, gesturing. "She is in pain, but there doesn't seem to be much that's been done about it."

Sallek moved her fine hands in the glimmer of their tiny fire. "She took an arrow in the lower calf," those hands signed. "A clean wound. Her companions cut away the ragged flesh and filled the cut with balm. She will not bleed again unless she has a fall or a hard blow to that area. She will never stop, and she will not slow our progress, if that is your worry."

She checked the mend and cut away extra leather, pulling the boot onto her stockinged foot. Lehnik gave a push to help her get it on; then he signed, "I am not worried about that. She would not have come if she thought it would hinder our mission. I simply hate for anyone to be in pain and to be unable to help her."

His fingers moved as if they were weary. Indeed, he was tired from head to heel, yet something was nagging at him and had been since they reached the hills. Unfriendly eyes stared down on them; he felt it in his gut.

An enemy of some kind waited beyond the next ridge. That was what his instinct told him, yet it was illogical. He tried to dismiss the fancy, as he rose to lay out his pack and unroll his blanket.

* * * * * * *

The Skerl waked them long before light touched the eastern sky. The creature nudged at Sallek, anxious and uneasy. Its feelings seemed to match Lehnik's own, the soldier thought, as he rolled his things together and caught the roan, which was cropping the grass close by.

The other Sisters were busy with their own mounts in the grassy glade where the animals had grazed overnight. A nosebag kept the animal quiet while he saddled the beast and secured his pack. Around him in the darkness he could hear the others moving, their horses snorting and stamping and munching their grain loudly.

At that moment, he heard something distant and obscure, yet still unmistakable to a soldier's ears. The clink of a muffled sword rang faintly against something metallic.

A hand touched his sleeve. Benthe had heard it, too. The Skerl must have felt the approach of men earlier than that, which must be why it had been so anxious to wake them into motion.

Warm breath fanned his ear, and Sallek's whisper said, "I will link with the Skerl and follow him. The other fully trained Sisters can link with me. You and Benthe must keep close to them, tethered to the last and to each other with these cords." She thrust lengths of line into his hand. "Kerrill will lead you.

"We go fast, for we have no time for skirmishing in these hills." She paused, her hand on his arm. The whisper came again. "It troubles me, Sister. No one should have or could have known we are here. No one except one of our own kind. But the Sisters of Silence want nothing any power on Halash can offer them." Even her whisper sounded strained.

"I think one of our kind has gone mad. The House of Garrouche was, remember, breached. That is no easy thing. With aid from inside it would have been far less difficult. Think on this." Then she was gone.

Lehnik looped the cord about his saddle tree with a knot that could not slip. He felt it tighten against his side as Benthe's mount followed. The roan responded to his knees, as he read the signals along the other taut span connecting him to Kerrill.

For a moment he heard the tiny purl of the spring at which they had watered. The horse grunted as it began climbing the steep bank beyond, and again the cord pressed tightly against his side.

This was like being blind, for the darkness was impenetrable. Even when his eyes adjusted, he could see only blacker bulks against slightly less black ones. Trees shut away the stars, and only the acute senses of the Skerl could have led the group away from their camp without mishap.

Lehnik felt no one could possibly follow the intricate path they were taking through the inky forest. No track could possibly be visible before daylight, and even by day he could tell from the lack of sound made by his animal's hooves that ages of leaf-mould were cushioning the steps of the horses. They must ride away from those who had come after them, free and clear...and then an unwelcome thought came into his mind. If a Sister rode with those behind them, no matter how mad she might be, she would be able to link with those who went before him.

She could follow Sallek as easily as Sallek followed the Skerl. No matter where they went or what they did to cover their tracks, still she would come.

Mad or sane, that Sister would inevitably find them. If she existed, she would follow, no matter what course they took.

CHAPTER FOURTEEN

Feeling obscurely uneasy, Lehnik followed the tug of the cord as the Sisters proceeded through the invisible forest. There was too much time to think and not enough to do, in such a situation, and he found himself considering his training and the behavior of the Sisters whose training was completed. He could think of nothing—neither torture, inducement, nor threat—that might have caused any Sister of Silence to forfeit her commitment to her own honor.

But might there be something else, some drug or herb or mental stress that might send a Sister mad? He thought hard, but it still seemed unlikely. Those who chose the Life had an internal balance and harmony that seemed to counterbalance insanity. Yet the nagging thought Sallek had introduced would not go away. There was something in it, he felt certain.

He heard Benthe's Janna stumble and grunt behind him, breaking his concentration. Glancing about, he found light touching the sky, very dim as yet but not quite the total darkness of before. He could see just a bit, though only shadows that gave his eyes something to work at. He could make out Kerrill and his mount just ahead of him, though he wasn't able to see anyone beyond that point.

After a while, the group paused to uncouple Lehnik and Benthe from the cord. Nothing was said, for all seemed to be in silent agreement that though their pursuers were probably far behind them, it was possible they might come more swiftly than expected. All of these people had known what it was to be pursued, and Lehnik knew that everyone's instincts were alert.

Anyone behind could follow only if led by someone capable of linking with these minds. Lehnik saw in the eyes of Sallek and Kerrill and the other three an awareness that a Sister was leading the search behind them. The thought made him shiver in the morning chill.

Now the Skerl made a snuffling sound, as if urging them to hurry. They needed no encouragement, following the small creature into a seemingly impenetrable thicket ending at a solid wall of stone. A stream trickled along the wall, and Sallek bent her thoughts upon the minds of the horses.

Lehnik thought she might be instructing them, for all stamped and whickered and moved away down the stream to disappear into the thickets. Lehnik could only surmise that the horses were taking an easy path, as their simple minds would not be followed by the Sister behind them.

Sallek bent and sidled into an invisible crevice. One by one, the other Sisters approached the spot where her grimy white figure had disappeared, found the cranny, and managed to pass through it. Kerrill had difficulty, but at last he emerged on the other side, bruised about the ribs and skinned as to his elbows.

Lehnik, though smaller than Kerrill, found the way a bit difficult, himself. He wondered how the big Sister had managed to thrust his wide shoulders through that narrow space.

Once on the other side, he felt they might have gained a bit on their pursuers. Even a Sister leading that party could not know about that opening, without a Skerl to guide her. The ones in his group were now shielding their thoughts closely, he knew, for he felt no moth-wing brush of question or reply brush past his senses.

Now they were on the downslope of a thickly forested hill. Slender conifers raised needled crests against the morning sky, and the floor of the wood was smooth, thickly padded with needles that had been dropped over many centuries. After a short wait, they heard the quiet sounds of hooves in mulch, and their horses appeared around a bulwark of stone.

They mounted and went after the Skerl, who was making good speed across this silent and grateful terrain. At the foot of the hill, they found a deep burn, shrouded with ferns and shrubbery. Its waters were clear and cold, but they swam their mounts across, shivering and snorting, to a half-submerged gravel bar on the farther shore.

There they walked the animals along in the edge of the water for several miles, as the meandering of the stream took the general direction they wanted. Eventually, the Skerl led them ashore and up through a tangle of logs and branches. Those had evidently been deposited there by the high waters of winter rains, but the debris concealed all traces of their passing.

Now the injured Sister gestured, and Sallek came back to stand in a huddle with her fellows, their hands flying. But once Sallek understood that Lehnik and Benthe were unable to understand the

111

hand-language motioned at such high rates of speed, she spoke aloud.

"We have felt back along our link with the one who follows," she said. "There is only one, we think, who guides those who come after us.

"Though only four came from Chelos to do this work, now we are seven. We have enough people to allow us to divide our numbers into two parties, each with the purpose of destroying the Elector's weapons.

"Those behind us can follow only one group, for their guide can focus only in a single direction. The group that is not followed can speed toward the Stronghold, which is now less than three days' journey from this point, if the journey takes no unexpected twists. We will hope that is a realistic estimate."

Lehnik nodded, thinking hard. "Good. If we split our group, I will lead the one that follows the recognizable paths, for I am only half trained, less useful to our mission than any of the rest of you. I have spent most of my life at dodging those who desired my death, and it is my strongest skill. I can avoid pursuers, I think."

He stared about at the thick forest. "If nothing else, I can keep them wandering in the trees for days, if only you can screen your minds so the Sister leading them at our heels cannot detect your presence. Can that be done?"

The wounded Sister limped to stand beside him. "It can be done. I will come with you, along with Sister Elie." She nodded toward the stockier of her companions. "We can emit exactly the same amount of mind-talk that the five of us were doing before we stopped.

"Those going toward Garrouche will damp their thoughts to nothing, speaking only with lips or hands. Our followers can have no idea that we have divided our number, while the Skerl leads the rest of us to the Stronghold by routes that will cut many hours from the journey. Is this to your liking?"

Lehnik bent his head. "Precisely to my liking," he murmured.

He turned to Benthe. "You are skilled as are few I have known at the arts of war, but even you will be astonished at the abilities of these Sisters. Yet they may need your knowledge of common warrior tactics and of the reactions of officers whom you may know or against whom you may have battled.

"I believe this was to be my original function as leader of this party. I give the responsibility to you. Good fortune go with you all."

He turned and mounted his horse. Once seated, he noted that his companions were also in their saddles and ready to go. His group was all mounted, needing maneuverability more than the more secret party, who would ride double by turns, as they went. He looked down with concern on those with whom he had ridden so far.

Benthe's eyes were twinkling above his grimy veil. Sallek's eyes seemed sad, but she stood stoutly, holding the rein of her black, on which the smallest of the other Sisters was already sitting.

Kerrill raised his hand, fingers curled in the old soldier's "battle and long life" signal. Lehnik smiled beneath his veil, for he had thought he recognized familiar patterns in the big Sister's ways of thinking.

Without speaking, he raised a hand, giving the farewell signal he had learned in his training at the House. Then he turned the roan's head toward the northeast, where he could see sunlight striking down into a clearing.

They rode out of the trees into full morning. Behind him, he heard the muffled thuds as his small group followed over the heavy mulch of the forest floor. He would have to take care not to leave tracks, he realized, for the Sister who followed would know at once if too few horses had passed where she led. Her training would keep her attention focused on the traces left by her quarry.

He signaled for the others to come in single file. That would make it more difficult to count hoof prints.

The clearing was crossed by a game trail, which led down to some loop in the stream they had left earlier. He followed it in the opposite direction, stooping flat in his saddle to avoid low-hanging boughs. In time the track became clearer and became a woodcutter's path. That, in turn, became a wagon track, which skirted a smaller brook before turning eastward.

He was satisfied that those he hoped to lead astray would think their quarry was overconfident. Such a belief might make them careless, if he was lucky and the officer in charge was young and full of the cockiness of inexperience. Yet he did not count on such good fortune. He had to behave as if he were followed by the most seasoned officer in all the armies of Garrouche.

He stopped when the sun was overhead, and they dismounted to rest the animals. The Sisters chewed hastily on leathery dried fruits and meat while they walked, but they said nothing, either by word or sign. Lehnik felt a strange dislike for speaking, but he knew he must ask questions of the new Sisters, Elie and Shira.

"Do any follow us?" he signed to Shira. "I have a strange feeling, though it might be nerves or illusion. I would hate to believe our pursuers might be following the others, instead of us."

Shira stopped in her tracks and handed her reins to Elie. She shook out her robes and sat on a tree stump left by the woodcutter. A small furrow appeared between her brow, above her veil.

Her hands moved. "They are far back. The wall of rock behind that thicket puzzled them for some time. It's clear that the Sister felt our passing there, but they could not decide what we did with the horses." She paused, hands stilling and eyes closing again. Once again, her hands moved.

"I can hardly feel the Sister who is with them, and that is a good thing. Those who followed the Skerl will be clear of her range by the time she comes to the burn."

Lehnik leaned to make signs of his own. "What of the Skerl? Can she know we have been guided by that creature?"

Shira smiled, the veil about her cheeks wrinkling to reveal it. "Only three of all the Sisterhood of Halash can link with Skerl. Only they can sense such a linkage. This is not one of those three, for we know them all and they are accounted for. She can have no hint of this connection." Her hands slowed, then sped again.

"The lack of such knowledge will make it likely for them to miss the others entirely. Our traces, our thought patterns are all she will sense, if we are lucky. Otherwise she would have to be a most unusual Sister, indeed."

Lehnik grunted softly. He didn't want to get too far ahead of those following, yet he had to make it seem this group was trying with all its might to elude any pursuit. He needed a convincing excuse for some serious delay in his journey.

He searched his imagination, only to come up with a single notion. "If there were an accident...," he mused aloud.

"Better than that! A re-injury," said Shira, also aloud. "She who comes behind knows I am wounded. The aura of my pain touches her thought, no matter how well I mask it. An accident that reopens my wound would be credible, I think." She glanced about.

"Perhaps if my horse fell...." She did not wait for his reply. She climbed onto the former pack horse, though the effort wrenched a groan from her, and touched her heel to his flank.

The beast trotted toward the game trail that led to the north from the clearing where she had paused. Lehnik realized she must have some special skill or linkage with animals, herself, for without any signal, as if trained for the trick, the horse went over onto one knee and rolled onto his side.

Shira pulled her knee out of danger just in time, but the quick motion, as well as the impact as she fell, must have been excruciating. Even Lehnik, dull as his perceptions were, could feel it. He knew the Sister behind them must have felt the full blast of pain that accompanied the injury.

Elie was beside her at once, pulling Shira away before the horse could rise again. The beast stamped, shaking his head and making a haze of dust that flew out of his dun-colored coat.

The Sisters moved onto a patch of grass, where Elie laid Shira on her cloak. The pain was all too real, Lehnik knew, as he looked into the packet of medications Sallek had placed in his bedroll. There was a pottery jar of healing balm.

Kneeling beside Shira, he examined her swiftly for broken bones. "You need not have done this so thoroughly," he said. "Surely a less painful accident would have been enough."

She gritted her teeth around the word *no*. "There could be no falseness. The one who comes behind is in a strange state—she seems hypersensitive to everything, as if she might be drugged." She knitted her brows and looked up questioningly.

"We can't be certain." He helped Elie clean away the bandage, dust, and debris from the reopened wound.

Shira sighed. "She would have known at once if I feigned any injury. Then she would wonder why we wanted for her to follow us. No, better to have pain now than to have our entire mission fail. Do you deny that you would have done the same?" Her gaze was quizzical over the dusty veil.

He sighed in turn, looking down at the bloody trickles of red running away into the grass. The original wound had not been a trivial one. He could see where the arrow had gone in from an angle, tearing skin and muscle as it went.

This new stress had torn open the scar tissue that had formed at the entry and exit points, undoing days of healing. But he cleaned the wound carefully with water from his bottle. Then he and Elie smoothed the balm into the wounds.

Once that was done, Elie took from her pack a fresh roll of bandage. "I have done this many times," she said. "You talk to her and take her mind from the pain, while I wrap the leg again."

He tried to think of something that might distract the Sister, as he settled onto the grass and took Shira's hand in his own. Her long fingers gripped his spasmodically, once. Then they relaxed, as she asserted her discipline.

Then he thought of something that had puzzled him during all the months of his training. "Tell me, Shira, why those who are not in the Order believe we are under some sort of terrible oath? I have been told, back in my soldiering days, stupid things like the idea that Sisters have their tongues removed to prevent any temptation to speak."

She chuckled painfully. "I know. I have heard things just as silly. Ours is such a simple life, and our choosing is so free from compulsion that I wonder myself how such misconceptions got about."

A crinkle appeared at the corners of her black eyes, as she smiled beneath her veil. "I have never really thought about it, for I chose as a child who had been taught in a House. The opinions of those outside were never considered, though once I was trained and began my work I saw such attitudes. I dismissed them as nonsense without a second thought."

Elie tightened the bandage, and Shira's hand clenched again about Lehnik's.

"I have worked and healed and taught and listened to the woes of those outside the Houses. They seem to live on a very physical level and I suspect they cannot conceive of anyone voluntarily turning her back on physical matters." She flinched, but he could see she was following her train of thought, now.

"What a deprivation it must be not to talk platitudes from morning to night. Not to lust after food or power or objects of passion—those are things beyond the comprehension of many of those I have known. They have to rationalize such a choice on our parts. They must find some overriding reason why we adhere to our decisions.

"They think we have to be orphans or have lost our only true loves or are ugly, or something of the sort. And even then, they believe that only the most stringent vows could hold anyone to such an 'unnatural' life, even though it is freely chosen." She chuckled again.

Elie looked up. "Do you remember, Sister Lehnik, what it was like lying in your cot at night while you were in training? All the thoughts scampered around your skull like insects in the leaves. Do you recall the questions you had to answer for yourself or go forever without any answer at all? How many do you know who could possibly restrain their desire to know at once and be content to wait to work out the answers for themselves?"

Lehnik sighed. "Very few. Perhaps Benthe. Perhaps one other who...did not live. I see your point. We are not like our peers in the world. Either there is something lacking in us, or there is something within us others lack. Whichever it is, it is something that holds us forever apart. Thank you, Sisters."

Shira glanced down at the leg, now completely bandaged. "I thank you, Sister Lehnik, for taking my thoughts from my leg. You are skilled at that sort of thing, and you are not, though you may think it, half trained. Speaker would never have chosen you if that had been true.

"Not one of us ever completes her training, no matter how long we may live. There are some things that would make your work easier, which you have not yet learned, it is true. Yet you hold within yourself the full discipline of a Sister. Never doubt it, and never deny it to yourself. A time may come when only such confidence will stand between your heart and despair."

Her eyes closed. "I must rest," she murmured, and at once she was asleep.

Sister Elie rose and reached to help him up. "She will sleep for two hours. That much will allow those behind to close the gap just enough, yet not too much."

"Then we should rest, as well," Lehnik said. "It has been a long ride, since the inn. I could use the rest, but I will watch for one hour, then wake you so I can sleep a bit myself."

He sat back against a tree trunk, keeping the grazing horses in view and listening to the mid-day forest. Some small beast scampered about in the treetops above him, knocking down bits of bark onto his veiled head. In the distance a cow lowed, and he knew there must be a farm beyond the wood.

A thousand tiny sounds came to his ears. He realized he had never before been capable of perceiving fully the affairs taking place in a forest. Was it his training? It could only be that, honing his senses as well as the part of his mind that attended to small details.

He could hear the quiet breaths of his companions. He could even feel the fever building in Shira's body, as she slept.

He straightened against the trunk. If she had been one of the soldiers among whom she had worked, that could be catastrophic. But once she understood what was happening, she would squeeze the fever out of her flesh with sheer will. He knew it, for he understood with sudden clarity that he could do it for himself, as well.

After an hour, he woke Sister Elie and took his turn at sleeping. Even as he dozed, however, some newly awakened sense moved back along the track over which they had come.

He felt, and his sleeping mind knew, the approach of that renegade Sister who followed them.

CHAPTER FIFTEEN

After precisely two hours, Sister Shira opened her eyes, sat up with a bit of effort, and said, "They are coming. It is time for us to go."

It took only a moment to catch the horses, restore the packs to their original positions, and ready themselves to move again. Lehnik lifted Shira onto her horse, though she protested.

"Save all the strength you can," he advised her. "We may need every bit we possess before we finish this task. There are still two days and a bit to fill with evasion and retreat before we can turn our steps toward the Stronghold."

Never had two days seemed so long and nightmarish. Although Lehnik had campaigned across the Kell after bandits and raiders, in past years, he had kept to roads, or at least passable wagon tracks. Large groups of soldiers tend to use the easiest routes possible.

Now he felt he was forced to learn every game trail, every woodcutter's path, and every smuggler's secret way in all the area from Kell to Stronghold. Fortunately, there were few farmsteads, and the thick forest was perfect cover for his small band as they struggled to tease their pursuers after them.

But he always felt, just a half-day behind, the persistent presence of those who followed. That made him feel more content with his lot, for it meant the other group must even now be approaching the Stronghold, if they had any luck at all.

On the evening of the third day, Lehnik abandoned any pretense at meandering and headed straight for their goal. Before his party lay a short stretch of forest and the shallow stream called the Klein-Kell, which fed into the river far to the west.

Across the stream there should be a straight shot toward the Stronghold, which stood halfway between Kell-Ford and Selni, the capital city of the Elector's realm. Lehnik hoped the journey would be as straightforward as the route, but being a soldier he doubted the possibility.

They took care to rest the horses often and to feed them well, knowing that there would be some need for speed and bottom at the end of the journey. Now the animals stepped out vigorously, glad to end the pointless wandering of the past days in the forest.

Lehnik was even more thankful. The real task was now at hand, though he asked himself often if the Sister leading their followers might not be suspicious of such uncharacteristic indecision and aimlessness on the part of her peers.

The group emerged from the trees onto a strip of sandy gravel. A scant dozen yards from the small river, they could see the waters of the Klein-Kell, still high along the banks because of recent rains. The water was swift but shallow, and they waded their mounts across after Lehnik rode the roan halfway and sounded the middle of the riverbed.

Once they were on the other side, he felt his heart lift. Now they could go arrow-straight toward the Stronghold, with some hope of lending aid to those who had gone before them.

Shira knew this country as one knows her homeland, for she had been born on a farmhold to the east. Her youth, until she was sent to the House of Silence, had been spent roaming at her brothers' heels across the grasslands and forests through which they must travel.

She took the lead, and now Lehnik could see no trace of pain or fever. Strangely, as he watched the way she handled her own physical problems, he found in himself the capacity to deal with his own. At the moment this was only fatigue, but it was like remembering something he had always known.

He could heal himself at need, he was certain, and the ability had always been there. It was simply that few understood its presence or how to use it. Watching Shira had roused the old capacity inside him.

Riding in Shira's wake down a long glade, Lehnik felt wide awake, alert for danger, yet it left another part of him free. Something inside him was opening out, saying to him that all possessed the abilities to become a Sister, hidden away, unsummoned and untrained.

That reassured him, for he had wondered if he were beginning to feel superior. Something in his character was uncomfortable with such arrogance, and if his capacities were common to all, he had no excuse to boast of them.

He fell slightly behind, watching the back trail as he moved across the meadow. Shira rode into the forest at the other end, followed by Elie. He gave a long last look at the edge of the forest be-hind them before he realized he had committed a fatal error.

A bow twanged. He dropped flat in his saddle, but he was too slow. The arrow caught him high in the muscle of his back, angled toward his shoulder. He kneed the horse to a gallop, but he avoided the spot into which Elie had disappeared. Those two could do the work without him, he knew. He must cover their trail.

Hooves pounded behind him from the stretch of woodland. He turned to see how near his pursuer might be...and blackness fell over him like a blanket. Even as he fell he heard voices, but he had no time to distinguish words.

* * * * * * *

Lehnik came to himself in a blaze of pain, lying on his stomach on the ground. His cloak seemed to be bunched beneath his cheek, and some demon was at work on his back with red-hot tongs. Then he woke fully and realized that a practiced hand was removing the arrowhead from his back. Skill, he knew for the first time, did not mean painlessness. He controlled a groan.

A lump over his right ear, throbbing foully, was almost pleasure by contrast.

"Be still," said a gruff voice. "I'm almost done with you."

Lehnik went still with shock. He knew that voice!

"Koreb?" he asked softly.

There were few voices with such a gravelly quality, and only one he had heard belonged to a military surgeon. The mercenary was from Horniche and had campaigned with Krohm's troops sev-eral years before.

"You've finally woke up, then?" said the voice. "Wondered how long it'd take for you to know me. I almost never knew you, got up like a Sister of Silence. Spying now, are you?"

Several replies ran through Lehnik's mind very quickly. It might be to the advantage of his fellows if he were thought to be a spy and not a real Sister, though the Sister who guided this bunch might betray him at any time. Still, it was worth trying.

He groaned. "Now did you ever meet a spy who'd admit to it?" he asked, as Koreb turned him on his side.

The surgeon chuckled. "Never did." Koreb lifted him carefully and set the rim of a cup to his lips. "Here, drink this. Make the jour-ney to Selni easier for you. We're going to move fast, now we've got you in hand. You led us a merry chase, you did. What in blazes was the point of all that lollygagging about in the woods?"

He laid his patient down again carefully, with a pack to keep him from rolling onto his back. "Your fellows got clean away from us, and our tame Sister can't seem to get a line on 'em, so we're going to make do with you. Too bad. I liked you."

Lehnik looked up into those tar-black eyes, the lined and leathery face. There was real concern there, and he recalled the soldiering they had done together, the long nights of talk in camp. They had, indeed, formed a bond of friendship.

He need not fear that Koreb would poison him, particularly if he was to be taken in for questioning. He sipped at the bitter brew, feeling it burn all the way down his gullet. Once again the black wave engulfed him, drowning the fire in his back.

* * * * * * *

When he woke, it was to find himself tied onto a horse. His own? Yes, he knew it by the gait. He was fastened astride, his legs secured with saddle-straps. His face rested against the mane of the horse, right cheek down. He risked opening one eye a crack, and that allowed him to see the rump of a black near the shoulder of his own mount.

Someone was leading the roan. He could hear many other hooves crunching the gravel of the road, and from the sound and the rapid flex of his horse's body he knew they moved at a trot. Koreb had not lied when he said they would make speed, but something inside told him they did not ride to Selni. If he was not badly mistaken, it was to the Stronghold the troop was hurrying.

The wound in his back felt like a rod of fire, laid across the muscle and skin. Yet he was able to hold it at a distance, keeping it apart from his mind. He would have smiled, but for the fear of betraying his consciousness. The training had done that, leaving the mind free, set apart in a place to which neither fear nor pain could come.

His mind was clear to read his present circumstances logically, without the pressures of emotion. He could also concentrate on healing his body, making it ready for whatever waited at the end of this journey.

Closing his eyes, Lehnik relaxed, flowing with the gait of the animal. He visualized crystal-green waters of healing running through his flesh, carrying away any poisons or infections, making new flesh to mend the old. Sharp twinges prickled around the wound. Itches, burnings, told him his new-found skill was working its magic. He could almost feel his muscle knitting back together, although he knew it could not work that fast.

After a time, despite his awkward position, he slept. He woke to find the troop walking the horses and slept again, blessing Koreb's drug.

That went on for a whole day, and when he woke fully at last it was to find himself in a night camp. Koreb appeared to untie him, lifting him off the horse.

Lehnik found his feet were numb and had forgotten how to stand. His legs seemed limp, as if filled with water. It was only with the surgeon's help that he made it to the spot where his bedroll had been spread.

He sat, breathing deeply, for some time, feeling disoriented and dizzy. The pain in his back was appreciably less, for which he was thankful. When he flexed his shoulders, only a deep thrust of agony skewered him. The starburst of pain that had surrounded the wound was no longer there. Satisfied, he kept a part of his mind concentrated upon completing the healing process.

A very young soldier brought a bowl of boiled beef, after some time. Lehnik ate with more determination than appetite. Cheese and hard bread followed the beef, and he could feel the food reinforcing his internal efforts.

Koreb came to look at his back. That was something he would have avoided, for there was no way for the surgeon could miss what was happening. But there was no help for it, though he would have preferred to leave his captors in ignorance of his true condition.

"Go over on your face," the gruff voice ordered. "No way to see, with you sitting up. Boy, bring the torch!"

The light came near as Lehnik rolled onto his stomach Koreb pulled up the tail of his grimy robe and began unwrapping bandages around his shoulder. There came a tearing and tugging as the blood-soaked material pulled free of the wound. Wet swabs touched his skin, sending chilly trickles down his backbone.

"By steel and starlight!" came a startled exclamation from the surgeon.

"Boy, you stick that torch in the ground, yes like that, and go see if someone wants you. I can tend to this well enough. The Kaporal was looking for you, just now."

Lehnik lay tense, waiting as fingers moved on his back, swabbing, anointing, rebandaging. Then Koreb said, "Well, now, it appears that you be no spy, after all. But you're not a woman, either.

"The Teachers of the Spirit are always going on about the Sisterhood of Silence being a bunch of women who want to put down and subjugate men. But only they could have healed themselves as you are doing. And you're as male as they come. That is strange."

Koreb caught Lehnik about the shoulders and helped him to sit. Then he finished wrapping bandages around chest and shoulder and arm.

"There's nobody near enough to hear," the burly surgeon said into his ear. "And I've no love for these new employers of mine, though I do have regard for you, as an old comrade in arms. Tell me what you can. I might be of help to you, though not openly and in defiance of my contract, of course. Perhaps by a bit of slovenly work at a crucial time, eh?"

Lehnik grinned beneath his veil. "Do any others know I am not a woman?" he asked softly.

"I kept that to myself, particularly once I knew who you are. I figured they'd find out in good time, anyway."

Lehnik felt great relief. "Good. Koreb, my friend, some half of all the Order of Silence is made up of men. I couldn't give you a precise number, for it isn't often you know for certain which of your Sisters is male and which female. But it's half, or near enough.

"Until less than a year ago, I was still Krohm's Master of Horse. He sent me on an errand to the House of Silence, and there I found something I had needed, without knowing it, for all of my life. They arranged for my release, and I trained among them. Now I am a Sister in good standing."

"Whooo," breathed the big surgeon. "Half, you say? That gives the lie to the Fraternity, all of whom are men and all of whom hate women, except for raping them or working them to death. They're the ones who have the ear of the Elector, you see. They think he'll put power in their hands, once they have the control of Trans-Kell.

"They want to root out every House of Silence on Halash, over time, and I have decided they're using the Elector to establish their own power. Likely others like him, too, in other countries."

He chuckled softly. "I was with the troops in the Stronghold for a time, because of being a surgeon. I was called more than once to tend those in the Elector's personal guard. That slippery bastard knows just what the Fraternity is trying to do. He laughs at 'em, even while he uses 'em for his own ends. They'll get no power from him, believe me. That's no secret among his guard.

"Those are tough, skeptical men, every one of them. They've no use for the Brothers who come tagging after them, trying to convert them to their beliefs. Most of those men have wives and sisters and mothers who take care of their businesses and farms while they put in their stint at soldiering. They know their womenfolk can be trusted, whatever the meechin' Brothers may say." He laughed aloud and poked the fire.

"I've seen 'em all but spit in the Brothers' faces. It's a joke in the barracks, when the men discuss the Elector's long-term aims."

"Hmmm." Lehnik turned his head to look into those tar-pit eyes. "Then why is the Elector invading Trans-Kell? He has no need of more land. His own country is only half populated, and ours has even fewer people. There is room and to spare on this world our ancestors found for us."

"You may guess, and I may guess, but my best guess is that even the Elector doesn't know for certain. He's a bored little man, tired of life in the Stronghold. He's made enemies of his own people and can't risk himself outside the citadel without an army in attendance.

"He's trapped himself, and he needs something to interest and challenge him. He's intelligent. Too intelligent to make the mistakes he's made, actually."

Lehnik nodded, thinking hard. How far could he trust this old comrade? His instinct told him Koreb was sound to the core, but he had learned caution in a hard school. He decided to probe for information before entrusting any hint of his task to the Hornichean.

"Has there been any talk of the House of Silence in Garrouche being breached?" he asked, watching a file of troopers tramping along with firewood toward the main campfire. He carefully did not let his expression reveal anything except casual interest.

Koreb, too, watched the wood-carriers until they were out of earshot. Then, cleaning and putting his instruments into their bag, he said, "A rumor. Just a rumor, but it came with another rumor about powerful weapons that have come into the Elector's hands. And now we're led by a Sister, though that is something any of us would have sworn to be impossible, after the breaching of her House."

He glanced aside at Lehnik. "I am not allowed near her, which is a bit unnatural. But by watching from a distance, I'd say something is wrong with her mind. She doesn't seem normal, even for a Sister.

125

"Most of the mercenaries and all of the Garrouche troops are uneasy. The Sisters have been our friends always, no matter where we fought or on what side. They have been the only trustworthy people both sides could rely on. The thought of messing about with the Order is a disturbing one. Thinking about drugging one of them into our service is almost blasphemous."

Lehnik decided to trust his own instinct. "There are weapons in the Houses that are too dangerous to put into the hands of anyone, far less a bored Elector. They were left in the custody of the Sisterhood, stored in the Houses of every country on Halash.

"Now the Elector has seized those in Garrouche, but even he is not stupid enough to use them indiscriminately. He is trying traditional warfare first. If he is unsuccessful with that, he will use the items he has stolen. Those could destroy all of Garrouche, all of Trans-Kell. Possibly this entire continent, which is the only sizable land-mass on this world. Nothing would be left to rule, and nobody would be left to rule it.

"I was sent with others to destroy that arsenal." He looked sharply at Koreb, who closed his bag and strapped it tightly. "The Elector himself has no idea how powerful and dangerous those weapons are, and now he has no Sisters to advise him."

Koreb stood, motioning for Lehnik to lie down. A Kaporal was coming toward them.

"You just rest quietly now," he said. "The wound isn't mortifying, so you're lucky there. Sleep well, Sister. The potion I gave you should help you rest." He turned toward the Kaporal, who glanced down at Lehnik's veiled and swathed shape with much interest.

"She going to be all right?" he asked the surgeon. "A Sister helped my Mam when I was born. She'd have died without. I don't feel right about keeping one captive, no matter what the orders are."

Koreb put his bag into the young man's hands. "This Sister is going to be fine. No question about that. You can even wager on it, but I don't know about the other one."

One of the Hornichean's dark eyes was visible to Lehnik. The eyelid flickered quickly, then Koreb turned and followed the Kaporal away into the darkness.

CHAPTER SIXTEEN

As Lehnik had guessed, part of the troop turned at last from the main road to Selni, taking the broad way leading toward the Stronghold. Half their complement did continue toward the Capital, but Koreb accompanied the sizable group counted off to deliver their captive and their Sister-guide into the Elector's hands.

The surgeon had not removed the bandage from the arrow-wound since the first night of Lehnik's captivity. He assured his old companion that his own efforts were doing it more good than all the medications in his bag.

"There is no need to risk exposing you to any chance eye that might notice more than we would like," the burly man told him.

Lehnik agreed fully, for the wound seemed to be healing rapidly and relatively painlessly.

It seemed Koreb had led his officers to believe his captive's condition was very serious, and Lehnik had carried out the lie as well as he could, swaying in his saddle, appearing weary and ready to drop by the time they camped each night. He even allowed himself to come near to slipping from the saddle once or twice, though he was tied firmly with the saddle-straps and knew he would not really fall.

Between the two, they persuaded the Master of Horse that constant medical care was imperative. Koreb, therefore, was assigned to ride beside the captive, steadying his patient from time to time and keeping his professional eye upon this valuable prisoner.

Only once before had Lehnik visited the Stronghold, many years before when Krohm led a delegation from the Council to the Elector. He had been twenty, then, a common trooper of Horse, but he had been curious about the old city and had taken the opportunity to examine the place carefully, when his duties permitted.

Those colonists who had been planted in the lands that became Garrouche had built the Stronghold as one of their first projects. They had feared predators, Lehnik thought, in light of his tutoring in the House of Trans-Kell. There had even been a record in which they expressed fear of intelligent and possibly hostile native inhabitants.

Now Lehnik knew they had been correct, insofar as intelligence was concerned, but the colonists had not recognized those native people they met. So they had built strongly, intending their city to repel any attack and to last for millennia.

As the troop rode between the heavy gates, he saw again those thick sandstone walls. Beyond the first gate, which was set at a corner of the square forming the citadel, there was a wall, which forced incomers to turn left, then right, then left again, each time passing through still another gate. It was like a maze, and invaders could be attacked from the inward-leaning catwalks along the tops of the barriers.

Once past the last gate, there was a complex of streets running parallel to the outer walls. No entrance of any street aligned with that of any other, creating a further maze. At the center was the House of the Elector, and Lehnik found as they traveled through the confusing network that he recalled the way perfectly. Nothing had changed in the past fifteen years.

The streets were busy with many sorts of people. Garrouche drew its population from the judicious mix of races whose seeds had been planted by the colony ship, and even after so many centuries the old distinctions, brown and black, yellow and white, kept strong traits of their original heritage alive, though many khaki-tan skins reflected the mixing of kinds.

Lehnik thought of Speaker, with her smooth black skin and onyx eyes. He saw few as uniformly dark as she, but several came near it.

At last the troop drew up facing the Elector's gate. Three ancient men came out of the dark doorway and stood peering through the ironwork at Lehnik and his captors. They seemed to be arguing among themselves, but while they argued the Sister who had guided the troop was taken away to a side gate and from there into the building.

One of the oldsters came forward and said to the sergeant in charge, "Bring her into the Armory. You...."—he pointed to Koreb—"Come with her. For now."

The surgeon loosed the straps and a trooper lifted Lehnik from the chestnut, with great care. A youthful voice whispered into his ear, "Good luck, Sister. Forgive me."

Then Koreb's strong hand gripped his elbow, guiding him into the corridor behind the thick double doors. When the surgeon's hand withdrew, something long and keen slid beneath the bandage on his right arm. Lehnik held it tightly to his side as troopers helped him to a chair in a dark little chamber, where there was a table holding a jug of water and a plate of bread.

Those who had brought him withdrew. So did the old man who had accompanied them. He was alone, and at once he hid the slender blade in his tunic, beneath his robe, and secured it with the manifold sash that the Sisters used for many purposes.

As he ate, pretending to be slightly dazed, he tested out his body, flexing muscles, moving fingers and feet. He found himself in better condition than he could possibly have hoped. The wound was barely sore at all, and he now had free use of arm and shoulder, though he made certain that anyone watching through some peep-hole would not know he was testing out his body.

There was no fever. He felt clear-headed and alert; indeed, it was an effort to maintain his pose of sickness and exhaustion.

He was fit, and he had a weapon. He had been brought, as quickly as possible, to exactly the place where he had wanted to be. The rest of his group must have reached the Stronghold some time ago, and Shira and Elie, given any luck, would have found them and joined forces.

Either Sallek or Shira, he was sure, would be able to detect his presence, even at a distance. They would find him; it only remained for him to wait. There would be some opportunity to escape, perhaps, and if not he would trust the Sisters to break him free.

He finished his stingy meal and pushed away the dish. Almost at once, the heavy wooden door opened and the three graybeards re-entered the room. A Teacher of the Spirit accompanied them, his eyes watchful in the glow of the lamp they brought. He seemed to expect trickery or treachery from this wounded Sister.

Instant dislike welled up in Lehnik. This disturbed him, for it was no longer normal to feel such things. The training of a Sister wiped away those matters, and few outsiders were able to trigger such responses in him any longer.

The most feeble of the old men came to Lehnik and looked down at him with interest. "Another one. This will be most useful. With her, too, under our control, we may be able to slip an agent into the very Council of Trans-Kell. The drugs worked well on the first; let us try them on this one."

129

His tone implied this was not a human person but some lesser being, unable to understand his words. Lehnik might have been an animal or even a chemical experiment, interesting but without mind or feelings. This old man did not understand even his own humanity, Lehnik thought.

The Brother, standing behind the others, chuckled dryly, as if in agreement.

One of the other two raised a protesting hand. "We have been warned, Kale. Those drugs are unknown quantities, untested even upon well people. Would you risk killing this valuable captive before she is well enough to be of use? Remember what the Elector told us. We must go cautiously, for the things from that store were withheld because of the dangers they posed.

"The Order of Silence did not use them itself, which should tell us something about their potencies. No, I say cure her. Then drug her into our service."

Kale snorted, but he turned away. The second of his peers put a hand on his sleeve and nodded. "Lept is right. Sisters are not so easily captured alive. We cannot afford to risk this one, and a week should not harm our purpose. It may well see her become strong enough to try the drug."

Kale shrugged before stamping out of the room. All except the Brother followed him. This Teacher of the Spirit was thin, over-tall, but stooped like a fish-hook. His hair was the same nondescript gray as his eyes, and his skin was the khaki color of crossbreeding.

He moved silently to Lehnik's side and stood looking down. He did not touch this Sister, but his expression was filled with loathing. "Sister! hah! I spit upon all your kind," he whispered.

"You turn the commoners from our teachings and away from our service. Your constant silence seems to hold more weight with them than our deepest teachings. You are trusted as emissaries and advisors by those who rule here, while we are pushed aside as a lesser Order.

"You will pay for that, on behalf of all your Sisterhood. I will see to that, *Sister!*" He strode from the room, and only the swish of his garments betrayed his going.

So. What had the Brothers been up to, that the rulers of most countries no longer trusted them? Had it been their influence that corrupted the Elector? Had it been their machinations that brought about the breach of this House?

Though once he would have found the thought far-fetched, he now felt it likely. The Teachers of the Spirit in Trans-Kell had possessed a good name, always, but that did not mean they did everywhere.

He glanced up to find Koreb standing in the doorway. The Teacher, interrupted before he could fasten the door, paused to look him over, seeming to note his insignia and the green tunic that denoted his service.

"You are the surgeon who attends this person?" he asked, his voice acid.

"Yes, Brother, I am." Koreb was not one to be intimidated by anyone, far less one of the Brothers.

"Why have you not been sent about your duties? Another surgeon can now be assigned this unpleasant duty."

Koreb's face assumed its innocently aggrieved expression. "I would like to tell you the answer, Brother. I asked to be allowed to return to my troop and be quit of this duty. I made the request all the way up the line of command and went through the Hall of Military Affairs. They all seem to think that I have begun the job and have to keep it, no matter what happens to those who are my true responsibility."

The Brother relaxed. A bitter smile touched his lips. "Ah, yes. It is often so in the military, I understand. Do your duty, Surgeon." He stalked away as if satisfied the prisoner was in properly hostile hands.

Lehnik, listening silently, was hard put to keep from laughing aloud. Any rank recruit learned quickly the one certain way to get a duty: pretend to hate it and try to avoid it. Or, of course, the reverse.

Something about the military mind-set looked with suspicion on the desires of those caught in its toils. Koreb had managed to stay with him in a manner totally above suspicion.

When the door closed behind Koreb, Lehnik let himself chuckle silently, though the vibration sent small lightnings of pain through his wound. Koreb came close, and they laughed noiselessly together.

At last he said, "Well, we're here. You feel like walking? I'll help you up. We must go to the quarters they have ready for you. Plenty of locks, mark you, and bolts on the outsides of every door between here and there. Don't think you will escape from this place, even when you feel much better than you look now. Here." He pretended to heave Lehnik roughly to his feet.

They moved slowly down the corridor, Lehnik leaning convincingly on the doctor's shoulder and dragging his feet as if unable to lift them properly. Nobody took any notice, and they turned at last

131

into a cross corridor leading to a dead end. Three metal-studded doors faced them, right, left, and at the end of the hallway.

Koreb opened the one on the left with a massive key. This revealed a fair-sized room, walled in stone and seeming to have been hollowed out of the hill on which the Stronghold sat. The sandstone was seamless, reminding him of the hold of the Harveem. Here, however, chisel-marks showed the stone had been smoothed by hands.

Lehnik pointed to the grillwork above the door and raised his eyebrows. Koreb nodded. Then he led his patient to a high couch in one corner. There he examined the wound for the first time since that first night.

"You are almost healed," he said, his tone quiet but not too cautious. "Better than I could do for you."

Lehnik glanced at the wall. "Won't we be overheard?" he whispered.

The surgeon laughed. "This is the room they use for madmen and people whose tongues have been removed. It has no listening-holes. That grill is for air and occasional inspections. They don't expect to hear any talk here. They truly believe the Sisters can't talk at all, or else have sworn such a terrible oath they'd rather die than speak."

He offered a hand. Lehnik hauled himself into a sitting position. "That's a relief. I thought I was going to burst when you went into that performance for the Brother. It's easy to see he's never been a soldier."

"Or a farmer or builder or anything else useful," Koreb growled. "You in Trans-Kell haven't seen the changes happening among the Fraternity in most places. They've become power-mongers, if you have the wit to watch what they have been doing.

"In Horniche, we've banished the Order entirely. Our Hierarch may not be the best ruler on Halash, but she's no fool. The Brothers stopped choosing for their ranks anyone who does the work of the world. They began recruiting only the sons of the rich and powerful. Once they felt they were in position, they began trying to manipulate the Hierarch's policies at home and her dealings with other countries." He laughed again.

"She squashed them, of course. Half those in Garrouche are refugees from Horniche. They didn't find a welcome in Trans-Kell, so they kept coming here. Yours in Trans-Kell is the only group left that isn't entirely corrupted, as far as I can see."

Lehnik stared at him. "But why do they hate the Sisters? We have no interest in that sort of power-brokering, and we haven't any hidden purposes. We're open to anyone who can endure the training and the silence. We are just what we seem, and no more. It puzzles me."

Koreb grunted. "But they're *not* what they seem. They can't believe anyone is, d'you see? They think the Order has to be waiting for its chance to seize control of this world. When they found those weapons in the House, it didn't change their minds a bit, I'll wager.

"If the Sisters hadn't used the things, it had to be because they were saving them until the time was right for a takeover. I helped to clear out Horniche. The Hierarch's troops found a lot of interesting records, and we heard a lot more rumors that may or may not be true."

Lehnik sighed. "How like them," he said. "How like most people, for that matter. They suspect everyone of their own faults. But now I have a problem of my own. What do I do now?"

"Just wait," Koreb said. "You're almost well. There's a horrendous scar, and the wound still seeps a bit, so even if they send another surgeon to check, you can fool him, if you behave as if you're very weak and in considerable pain. He'll believe you. I can hardly believe you're not, in fact. Your training must be incredible, if it gives you this sort of control."

Lehnik gazed at him, assessing him for the first time as a possible candidate for the Sisterhood. "You might be a good Sister yourself, if you decide to give up soldiering. If you want something different to fill the rest of your life, it's quiet. Deep down, where you live, it's peaceful. You have time to think about everything you ever wanted to examine but put off for lack of time.

"You can get acquainted with the person you really are, down past all the habits and shams and self-delusions. Get in touch with your mind, actually. It's fascinating to watch it working away, unraveling the answers to questions you can't ask, and if you asked them nobody would answer."

Another wrinkle appeared between Koreb's eyes. Keen interest gleamed for an instant. Then he sighed in his own turn.

"That is a thought to keep with me. But for now I'd best finish my examination and get back to quarters. I expect the Elector will ask me for a report very soon, now." He stared down at Lehnik's white-clad form. "Believe me, Sister, if I had known about the Elector's plots before I took service with him I'd have stayed in Horniche or Trans-Kell. Back home we have roads that need repair, and that's the family business; did I ever tell you that?"

He laid a hand on Lehnik's shoulder. "You rest now. I'll see you in the morning. They claim there's no way to escape from this part of the Stronghold. I'm betting on you." Then he was gone.

Lehnik smiled behind his veil, lying back on the couch. There was a lot of thinking to do before morning came. He had best get busy with it.

CHAPTER SEVENTEEN

Lying in the darkness that filled the stone room after Koreb took away the lamp, Lehnik felt the flutter of sensation in his mind that meant contact with his Sisters. It was unfortunate he had no real talent in that direction, for it would have been easy to make plans, if he had the capability. But if nothing else, the feeling told him at least one of the Order was near. Where one was, others would also be found.

He straightened his limbs, folded his hands on his chest, and set his mind on his next move. It would be good, he felt, to take a part of the week the elders promised him for completing his recovery. Two days would be enough, unless something pushed him to speed up his plans. Astonishing as his recovery might be, it was always possible to suffer a setback, and he felt it best to avoid that, if possible.

Two days of rest and food would see him in fine fettle again, if they would feed him decently and refrain from drugging him. And then—he could only wait to see what would come next.

Before Koreb took the light, he had studied this room. Square, solid, its ceiling eight feet above the floor, it had no window and only the single door and the air grille. He was certain his first impression had been correct; the wall into which the door was set was cut from blocks of granite. The door itself was made of heavy wooden baulks, secured with iron bands and studded with rivets. Even the fist-sized peephole was barred.

The ventilator was level with the ceiling in the corner to the left of the door. Round, only some ten inches across, it gave the only air that supplied the room when the door was shut. In the dim light of the room, it had seemed to him even that small opening had a set of bars fastened crosswise.

He closed his eyes and relaxed, allowing crystal-green waters of spirit to flow through his mind and bear away all trace of fatigue and injury. He went into the silent depths he had discovered inside himself, feeling refreshed as he did so. He had not had the chance in days.

Cool, white, austere...he drifted out of his body for a time, into a place where all was calm and order and endless peace.

A sudden sound jerked him out of that well of silence. It was still very dark, a pale glimmer marking the position of the peephole in the door—he suspected there might be a watchlight in the corridor. He could see nothing, but there had been an unmistakable sound.

Concentrating, he found his straining ears picking up a scritching, soft as a mouse in a wall. A quiet panting—where had he heard something similar to that? There was a muffled thud, as of something small dropping onto the stone floor.

The Skerl? It was small enough to negotiate even the limited opening in the ceiling.

He sat and lowered his feet to the floor. Something with spiky fur touched his ankle, and he almost jumped. He lowered his right hand slowly, not trying to catch the creature, just letting it know his hand was near. A small, cold nose touched his palm.

He sighed. If the Skerl had been sent here, it must be for some purpose he could not yet perceive. He could not link with the creature, as Sallek had done. As far as he knew, it could not understand human language. Yet if it linked with Sallek, then the Sister could hear anything its small ears picked up. Perhaps *she* could hear him.

The bristly shape leaped lightly into his lap, put its head against his hand and went still. "Sallek? Can you hear me?" he asked.

The small head pushed into his hand, bobbing. So. She was able to pick up his words through the senses of the Skerl. Sitting in the dark with the little alien in his lap, Lehnik began to talk.

His report began the moment his group left to perform their misleading action and followed faithfully to the present. He gave a detailed account of Koreb and the surgeon's secret aid, as well as the binding oaths a mercenary must take.

Everything he could recall of his first visit to the Stronghold, all those years in the past, came out. He described the three elders and the Brother who had been with them. All he could wring from his disciplined memory, he poured into the Skerl's stiff-pointed ears.

"I will wait for two days, unless you want me to move earlier," he said at last. "Can the Skerl move his head if this is what you want?"

The small head jerked sideways against his palm. There was no necessity for him to move, yet.

136

"Then I will try the lock of this door with the blade Koreb gave me. Failing that, I may try enlarging the hole through which the Skerl came to me. I will get out. It might even be Koreb will suffer a lapse of memory and fail to double-lock the door."

The Skerl's ears twitched in his fingers, as if it tried to tell him something. He could feel tendrils of thought tickling about in his mind, but he could gain no meaning at all.

The creature bumped him with its head. Then it jumped to the floor, and he could hear, now that he knew what to listen for, the almost inaudible "*fuf-fuf*" of its paws on the gritty floor.

Again there came the scritching sound. How did it find places to fix its claws into the stone? There was a rustle as it squeezed through the ventilator. When it was gone, he felt suddenly lonely.

Lying back, he closed his eyes. Elation surged through him. If the Skerl could come to him undetected, then others might do the same.

He withdrew into white silence and rested there until the first light of day crept through the vent hole. That meant it had to open into the outside air, he thought. The end of the corridor must come at the outer wall, and that door had to lead out, as well.

He rose to stand beneath the opening. He sprang high and hooked his left hand around the crossbar, which held firm in its sockets. No, he realized, there was no socket. It was cut from the stone, too, a part of the chamber. Beyond it a duct must have been bored into the solid rock. There could be no breaking that bar from its anchorage.

The mutter of voices outside his door sent him back to his couch. He slid beneath the thin blanket and turned his face to the wall, as the door creaked open. Then he turned restlessly and opened his eyes.

Lept stood there, along with one of his companions. Kale was nowhere to be seen. Lehnik hoped that the old man had been assigned to some other duty.

"Sister, face us. I like to see the eyes when I question someone. Even if they cannot or will not answer me." Lept's tone was civil but firm. Lehnik made a show of sitting painfully, easing his feet over the edge of the cot and onto the floor.

A trooper brought a pair of stools into the room, and the two elders drew them up to face the couch where the captive sat. This left Lehnik to stare at them for a long moment, while the soldier removed the waste bucket he had used and brought fresh water and a tray holding a covered dish.

"Your surgeon says you will need nourishing food for several days, in order to return you to normal. We will provide that, along with his services, for one week only. After that, we intend to take you into our own service, whether you agree or not. It would be much preferable for you to cooperate of your own will, believe me.

"We have already acquired one of your Order who chose unwisely. The drug required to keep her obedient makes her extremely ill. She still struggles against its effects and tries not to follow our orders. That makes it even worse for her as we increase the dosages."

The elder looked deep into Lehnik's eyes. Lehnik held effortlessly to his tranquility, knowing this man did not understand anything about the people he dealt with. One who could not help betraying her fellows was blameless. Pain was only pain. Death was only death. One who walked along the white corridors of his own spirit did not concern himself with either.

The elder seemed disturbed by what he saw in Lehnik's eyes. He turned to his companion and said, "Solm, will you persuade her? She is not listening to me. Or she is too stupid to understand what I say."

The third of the men was by some years the youngest of the elders. He had a tangle of reddish-gray beard and pale brown eyes that held a hint of strangeness in their depths. His manner was disgustingly cajoling.

"Sister, it is not our aim to make war against your Order. The Brothers who are urging us to do that are not in control of our policies. We have no desire to torture or to kill anyone, particularly the Sisters of Silence. You are known to be impeccably honest, and we respect you.

"Yet we are forced to do what our ruler orders. This is our dilemma, and we suffer along with those we...persuade. Still, we are *forced* to persuade them."

Lehnik almost laughed. Was this man trying to make him pity one who was engaged in torturing and betraying his own kind? Was a Sister of Silence supposed to weep for someone who had freely chosen the crooked road he walked? That seemed laughable.

He said nothing, betraying no emotion by so much as the twitch of an eyebrow or a narrowing of his eyes. The training he had received controlled far more than his tongue. It took over automatically when there was a stressful situation, and he was grateful for the fact.

Lept snorted, rising. "So we have another stubborn one!"

138

Solm smiled, but his stretch of the lips was not pleasant. "They are *all* stubborn, Lept. I have said that before. If we capture a thousand, which we will almost certainly not be able to do, they would all be the same. Anyone who can complete the training given their kind cannot be frightened by threats." He chuckled deeply.

"That makes it far more interesting to question them. It makes it satisfying to control them, in the end. I relish that."

A sick feeling rose inside Lehnik as he saw the avid glint in those pale brown eyes. Those were the eyes of a born torturer, and he knew he should have recognized it at once, for this was not the first of the breed he had met in his career.

Lept stared into his face. "One week," he said. He turned and moved toward the door. "Zelt, remove the stools!"

When the soldier had carried out the stools and locked the door, Lehnik lay back to think about what he had heard. Only one Sister was a captive. She had to be the one who had been forced, by means of drugs, to show these monsters the way to breach her House.

She must have been taken without warning as she went about some legitimate errand for the Elector. None of the Order could possibly have been taken alive and unwounded once the House had fallen. He added basest treachery to the list of crimes laid at the door of the Elector's people.

He turned to the tray the soldier had left. It held a covered bowl of broth with meat, a chunk of bread. That, with fresh water, made his meal, and he could feel the food reviving him. He would not need a week, that was certain, to return to his full strength. Two days would be more than enough.

Koreb arrived before he was done with the bread. "I see they took me at my word," he said, examining the empty bowl. "They'd have kept you on bread and water and wondered why you never grew stronger. Any other soul with a wound like yours would have died of it, my friend.

"The idiots! But that's the sort the Elector likes to have about him. That is why he has done the things he has. There's nobody to talk sense to him. Where does the fool think he will go after he takes Trans-Kell, if he manages to do that?

"Why should he go so far, anyway? He doesn't need the land, and he will be swarmed by those renegade Brothers, in time, demanding their reward for helping him with this ridiculous project."

Koreb sat on the edge of the cot and stared at his patient. "The word in barracks is that the war is going so well across Kell that the Elector has given these elders here more time to learn to use the new

139

weapons. He had formerly set the testing for planting season. Now he delays it until harvest.

"He may be making headway, for there is word out that he hires bandits to overrun the hill towns. This keeps the folk there too busy to organize into militia to resist the invasion."

"This doesn't surprise me," Lehnik said. "The bandits were doing well enough, unaided, in the last year before I became a Sister. Krohm had us all over the map, chasing them. Now with the army of Garrouche mixing into the problem, I shudder to think what may be happening on the other side of the river. However, I am relieved at the delay in trying those weapons. That gives me time...."

The surgeon grinned and shook his head. "Don't tell me a thing. Then I can't betray you, no matter what orders I get. I have absolutely nothing useful to say." He checked Lehnik's pulse, checked his pupils, and glanced at the bandages.

"You are doing well. I'll see you tomorrow."

He took the tray with him as he left, and again Lehnik lay back and thought hard. But this time instead of solving problems he drifted into sleep.

A grating at the door woke him. He must have slept for a long time, for the spot behind the vent was dark again. Something seemed to be moving beyond the peephole in the door, which was opening.

Lehnik came to his feet silently, his blade slipping into his hand from the sleeve of his robe. He edged along the wall, away from the cot, and was ready to jump the one entering the room when a hiss stopped him.

The faint light from the corridor showed a tall shape near the open door, uniformed in green that looked gray in the dimness. Big-boned, wide-shouldered...something about the figure reminded him of...Kerrill!

The strange, unveiled face beneath the familiar eyes smiled. One hand said, "It's time to go," while the other held out a dark cloak.

Lehnik slipped it over his shoulders, over his whites. He removed his own veil and cowling, as well, stuffing them into the wide pouch built into his Sister's robes.

Kerrill handed him a steel cap with a small feather attached to the crown. Once that was in place and a blade had been belted at his waist over the dark green robe, Lehnik was only another of the Elector's troopers, following at the heels of an officer.

The big Sister led the way into the corridor, peeped around the intersection, and strode out with complete confidence. Lehnik came behind, braced and blank-eyed, as he'd learned to do in his soldiering days.

They passed a sleepy sergeant on guard beside a lamp in the hallway. Beyond was a wakeful officer, who seemed to be struggling to keep from dropping an armload of paperwork.

They passed Lept, who was hurrying toward the wide doors leading out into the night-bound street. He glanced once at the pair and then away. No recognition or premonition touched his expression, as he watched his invaluable prisoner go past and out into the night.

Everyone knew beyond doubt that the Order of Silence was composed solely of women. Those were men and automatically beyond suspicion.

Lehnik found himself with an almost irresistible impulse to laugh. Only Kerrill's warning side-glance kept him from giving vent to it.

CHAPTER EIGHTEEN

The night was still. No breeze moved through the narrow streets of the Stronghold, and the stench of closely packed layers of humanity was strong in the spring air. Above the slot formed by the street, Lehnik could see the Shepherd's Crook, now well past its midnight position in the sky.

It was about five hours before dawn, as well as he could judge. There was time to do many things before the Elector's people discovered their loss.

They turned a corner into a midnight street, and Lehnik touched Kerrill's sleeve. As there was no light by which to see hand-talk, he whispered, "That other Sister...have you learned where they keep her?"

"They moved her to the Elector's house, across the way beyond the Armory."

Lehnik remembered that formidable block of buildings. He had caught only a brief glimpse of it as he was hustled into the Armory, but he knew it and its surroundings very well from his early visit to the Stronghold.

At that time, he had known one of the outbuildings was used for holding important prisoners. Now he asked, "Is she held in a small, square building at the southeast corner of the wall surrounding the gardens?" His mind was already busy.

"The one with walls as thick as the length of my arm. No windows. Only vent-holes like the one the Skerl passed through. Guards every place you look," Kerrill whispered in reply.

"Have you located the place where they are storing the weapons?" Lehnik persisted.

"Of course. Sallek has had the Skerl rooting around the Elector's house ever since we arrived. The little beast can go under the noses of guards or officers or the Elector himself, bold as you please. They pay no attention to it, for there are several in the House held as pets."

They paused to let a drunken trooper stagger past. As the fellow stumbled around the corner, Lehnik found he was holding his breath. If only the Elector had put his treasure of weaponry into the place Krohm had told him about, all those years ago!

Kerrill paused to look around the next corner, glancing up and down the dim street before he continued, "The Deep Keep is now walled with metal, guarded by an entire troop quartered in the cells outside a new and stronger inner door." He waited for a citizen to pass on the other side of the dark street before he went on.

"Even the Skerl couldn't get into that place. Yet Sallek is sure it is where the weapons must be. Only the things they have tested so far are in the Armory. Those of the guard I've become friendly with say only a single piece at a time is removed from storage, and when they are done studying it, it is returned."

"Any rumor about those things inside the walled keep? Who the troops are and from whose command?" Lehnik asked.

Kerrill grunted. "They do not keep anyone inside with the weapons. Even the Elector is afraid of those things. When they found that small animals died when exposed for too long to some of the crates, the soldiers almost rebelled. They refused to guard the stuff from anyplace too near it.

"The wall was built as much to protect the guards from the weapons as the weapons from outsiders. The Elector commandeered all the lead in Garrouche to use for building it. The elders found, by the way, that only lead would protect living things from the breath of whatever is inside those crates."

Lehnik expelled his breath at last. "Then I believe I can take us into the very deepest part of that Keep without being detected. We have to consult with the others, of course, and we have to see to our Sister who is held in the prison house."

Kerrill pointed along the next street, toward the right. There was a lamp standard some distance along the way, and his green-clad arm was a dim blur against the stone of the wall behind him. Lehnik followed him silently, the two hurrying along the back street to a shabby door.

Kerrill tapped once, very lightly, and the door opened, revealing no betraying light from inside. It closed behind them as silently as it had opened, and they moved in single file down a dark hall, their footsteps gritting on unswept stone. Another door sighed open and swished shut.

Light bloomed from an oil lamp, revealing five figures clad in green uniforms like those of the Elector's troops. Benthe was there,

143

appropriately enough as a sergeant. Shira, Elie, Sallek, and the other Sister from the hills wore the close-fitting metal caps and made tolerably believable soldiers in their bulky cloaks.

Lehnik sighed with relief. They had lost no member of their group, as yet. Small as she was, Sallek looked every inch the youthful drummer that her insignia indicated, and he approved. But when he glanced at Shira he was taken aback.

Her face, revealed for the first time, was a pale ivory oval. The eyes he remembered glowed with dark fires, and her beauty stunned him, for a long moment.

He had thought such feelings to be lost in the quiet whiteness that had taken up residence inside his mind, but now they roused again. He shook himself mentally—almost physically—before he could manage to greet his former comrades with proper enthusiasm.

But he kept glancing at Shira. "We need to disguise our Sister," he said at last. "She simply does not look like a soldier. The rest of us can pass muster, at need. I am amazed, in fact, that Sister Sallek looks her part so convincingly. But with Sister Shira we have a problem."

She smiled, and he felt his chest squeeze with something like pain. "This is my old home, here in the Stronghold," she said. "My family kept this house as a place of safety in unsettled times. My father would bring the family here, when war or bandits threatened.

"It has stood empty for years, though servants tend it and keep it in repair. It still holds clothing of many kinds. I will make myself inconspicuous, believe me." She sounded a bit sad.

Lehnik wondered if she had been one of those beauties who are victims of their own faces, bidden to live solely in safe places and kept from the harsher adventures she would have preferred, once she had passed her hoydenish childhood. That might be the reason she had chosen the Order, with its concealing veils and its silence.

His thought was interrupted by Benthe. "We have found the weapons, right enough. In a hole so closely guarded even the Skerl can't reach it. We've thought about everything short of burning the Elector's house, and it wouldn't burn anyway, being of solid stone. The Sister is in a place almost as hard to crack." He sounded despondent, quite unlike himself.

Lehnik touched the thick shoulder. "I was here before," he said. "I know the city and the House of the Elector almost as well as those stationed here, barring any drastic changes recently. Sit, and I will tell you about that visit."

144

The room in which they sat was furnished with sitting-cushions and thick mats, and in a moment they were sitting in a circle like children about a storyteller. Lehnik looked about at his Sisters, thinking that only a short year before he had, of this number, known only Benthe. Now these people seemed closer than his own parents had ever been, for they had been constantly occupied with their business and paid him little attention.

"We were sent here a dozen years ago," he began, "to negotiate a trade agreement between the Council and the Elector, who was, at that time, the present ruler's father. Krohm was entrusted with guarding the Sister who dealt with the leader of Garrouche, but we who accompanied her were only for show. At that time we were at peace with our neighbors across the Kell, for that Elector was a man of honor.

"Yet Krohm was a commander whose vision was long. He knew that rulers die, situations change, and danger is usually just over the next horizon. He understood a time might come when we would need deep knowledge of the Stronghold, inside and out. Krohm never wasted an opportunity."

Lehnik could see the young Krohm in the eye of memory. His black beard had already been bushy and aggressive, but it had, at that time, held no gray strands. Those eyes had burned darkly in Krohm's tanned face as he assigned Lehnik and two companions their task while in the Stronghold.

"You are youngest of our group," he had said. "Full of mischief, as I have suggested to the Elector's troops. Such young men probe into things, ask questions, make nuisances of themselves in general. And they learn things that might come in useful, in years to come when the whining adolescent in the Elector's House comes to power."

Lehnik was reliving the scene, now. "We stood in the room assigned to us, and as we were the most minor of guests it was high up in the House, above even those of the servants. It was hot, for the summer sun bathed the roofs just above us, and below the window ranged the irregular landscape of tiles and chimneys and vent-pipes serving the House.

"Krohm didn't exactly tell us what to do, but he glanced, most suggestively, out of our window at the unguarded expanses of roof. He did not need to tell us more, for we had been carefully chosen for just this task. We knew to keep eyes and ears open, to memorize any scrap of information that might be useful. We wanted to explore those enticing rooftops, to which our window gave us full and secret access."

Shira gasped. Benthe grunted. Lehnik grinned at both.

"We discovered a chimney stack leading right down into the bowels of the building, past many vents for air circulation, into the Deep Keep itself. So tight are the doors into the cell blocks that any captive must have air piped down to him or he would suffocate.

"Who would dream anyone could find a way down there from the roof of the Stronghold itself? Yet that was what we did, and we found other useful matters, as well. In addition, we located every possible concealed entrance into the House of the Elector. We made certain of it, though there are many of those, some so insignificant as to be forgotten by the people who live there."

"So," Sallek breathed. "Our task becomes easy."

Lehnik laughed. "Easy? No, never that, I think. I learned while I was in the Armory that Gorst is in command of the guard. I know Gorst of old. Though we may make our way into the House, up all the thousands of stair steps, past guards and servants and chamberlains and officials of all kinds, it will not be easy. If we survive to have children, this will be a tale to tell them, for if it is possible at all it will be incredibly difficult."

Benthe was thinking, his brows drawn together in a deep wrinkle. "We need a plan. A diversion, perhaps. Two teams, one to go after the weapons, one to free the Sister. Lucky we arrived with more manpower than we planned, or we'd be short-handed. What do you think, Sister Lehnik?"

To Lehnik's amusement, the word 'Sister' came out without strain or forethought. To the sergeant, it had become a natural form of address. If they both lived, Lehnik thought he might well bring the sergeant into the Order, if the man desired to become one of their number.

But he did not betray his thought as he said, "I agree, a diversion is desirable. I think you may be our best choice for the source of that diversion. Kerrill and Sallek and the other Sister can try freeing the captive, while Elie and Shira wait here to contact any Sisters who come after us, if we fail.

"I have only one concern. How can I destroy those weapons, even if I arrive in the storage area and stand beside them? I know they can cause terrible destruction over many miles of territory, if they are used, so I don't dare detonate or otherwise activate them. Surely Speaker thought of that, but she said nothing to me."

146

Benthe sighed. "She spoke to me. Here, take this." He thrust a device like a large egg into Lehnik's hand. There was a knob on one end, something like a protruding button. On the other end was a circle of coppery metal centered with a dot of silver that quivered with light.

Benthe pointed to the button. "You push this," he said. "Then get away as fast as you can. I didn't quite understand when she told me what this does, but what I got out of it was this thing shakes everything to pieces, down to dust. People, too, if they're nearby and not shielded."

Lehnik put the thing into a pocket of his belted robe. "I should have known Speaker would take no chance of harming the innocent," he said. "My only regret is that if I fail, those who come behind me must hunt out the correct route, hit or miss."

"Never fear," said Sallek. "The Skerl has agreed to come with you, and it will remember everything. Even if I should perish while helping to free our Sister, it will guide other Sisters to the proper spot. It understands far more than you dream, although it seems so docile and animal-like. When you leave this house, it will be at your heels."

Lehnik touched the heavy bulge in his pocket. "Even this is one of those dreadful weapons?" he asked.

Benthe shook his head. "Speaker said this is no weapon. It was designed to destroy weapons safely, without poisoning the atmosphere or the soil. It came from the store in the House of Trans-Kell and is one of the few whose uses have been carefully learned by every generation of guardians since the first. That shows how much our ancestors feared their own weaponry, doesn't it?"

Lehnik yawned and stretched himself on his mat. "Then we must sleep. We have part of this night and another day to pass before our work begins." He made the sign of peace, and Sallek extinguished the lamp.

The house was still. The white peace inside Lehnik's mind expanded, and he went into it, into rest, and presently he slept.

147

CHAPTER NINETEEN

A stirring in the room woke Lehnik, and he sat, rubbing his eyes. "How stands the sun?" he asked Benthe, who was quietly whetting his long knife on a strip of leather.

"Past midday," the sergeant answered. "I watched from the roof, for a while. It's high enough to give one a view above the houses around us. I saw a lot of movement in the streets. Mounted troops are riding out as if they mean business. Supply wagons accompany them, as if they go on a long, hard campaign. They all are probably headed for Kell-Ford to refit the invading forces moving into our country.

"I don't see any women in the market stalls around the Elector's house. Few clotheslines hold wash, and nobody is scrubbing their clothes at the public fountains. The civilians are uneasy, and with good cause."

The door opened, and an ancient crone crept into the room. She was stooped, fragile, her face almost hidden beneath a head-scarf with a veil. The eyes that showed were shaded by an overhanging bandage that sheltered them from glare, as if she suffered from weak and painful eyes. Her crutch thumped and gritted on the stone floor as she moved to pause beside Lehnik. He rose at once and offered his cushion for her to sit on.

She laughed, her voice clear and youthful, and Lehnik turned to stare, amazed at its vigor. "You did not know me, Sister Lehnik. Admit it! Did I not tell you that I would make myself unrecognizable?" She lifted the eye-shield, and he saw the eyes of Sister Shira.

He looked closely. While it didn't seem that her face was disguised, her appearance was completely changed by her skillful use of scarf and veil. She might have walked safely through any barracks-full of woman-hungry soldiers without risking any danger to herself.

She sat down on the cushion beside his, waiting with him and the rest for nightfall. They shared food from their packs, but no one seemed disposed to speak. Silence was a comfortable habit, into which those who had been Sisters for a long while sank gratefully. Even Benthe seemed quite content to exercise his thoughts instead of his tongue.

Lehnik wondered if every one of them might not be refining their plans, testing the suitability of strategies, discarding useless ideas and replacing them with better ones. It was more than probable.

Time flowed past seamlessly, without causing any one of the group impatience or frustration. All knew how to wait, the Sisters through their training, the soldier because that was the vital element of his trade. From time to time they would take turns going to the roof to survey the sky and the streets below. Each, returning, made the sign that meant *Peace. Nothing is happening.*

When Lehnik took his turn, he made his way confidently up the steep stairs, through the small dark door onto the roof. Twilight was beginning to edge over the city, and the lamps above doorways had begun to form pools of warm light in the shadowy streets. The spaces between grew blacker by the minute, as night swept softly over the Stronghold. The time was very near.

He returned to rouse his comrades to action. Shira brought a lamp into a windowless room and set it on a low table. Each of the original four brought out of a hidden pocket or pouch the item with which she had been entrusted by Speaker. Lehnik put the metal egg Benthe had given him beside the others and laid near it the odd object Speaker had handed to him before he left Chelos.

Sallek bent to examine it closely. "This is a device that explodes quietly but most effectively. Those of us who have worked with the powder compounded of sulfur, charcoal, and saltpeter will find it hard to believe an explosion can make so little noise, yet Speaker says this is true of that small bit of metal. It will make it easier for us to breach the thick wall and reach our Sister."

She glanced at the sergeant. "If Benthe's diversion can cover our activities, we may be able to free her before the guard realizes what is happening."

Kerrill's pair of silvery globes lay in the center of the table. "These make a thick smoke. Sisters often use them in dangerous situations, for they pose no threat to those the smoke engulfs. This conceals things best left unseen. Our group will take one, Lehnik the other. This can simulate a structural fire very well, and he may need that. So may we."

Benthe nodded, his eyes bright. "You have seen what I brought. Speaker told me that is the most dangerous item of all those entrusted to us for this expedition. Take care, Lehnik. It could shake down the entire House of the Elector, if you should activate it near the principal structural supports. Down in the bed-rock of the Deep Keep, it should do only what we wish. But if a wall higher in the building crumbles, then take care!"

Lehnik again took the thing Speaker had given him and looked at it quizzically. "I believe this should go with Benthe. It makes a great deal of noise, Speaker told me, with many smaller explosions following the first. It peppers its surroundings with pellets of light stuff that also explode on impact. A wonderful thing for a diversion, I should think." He handed it to Benthe, who chuckled as he pocketed it.

Each chose an item suited to his purposes, along with a bit of dried fruit and meat from the combined store from their packs. It would be night, now, in the maze of streets outside Shira's house. The time had come to move.

Lehnik turned to lay a gentle hand on Shira's shoulder. Elie touched her fingertips to his, as did Sallek and the other Sister and Kerrill. Benthe spread his burly arms and hugged his old friend close, without speaking.

Then Lehnik, who had the longest distance to travel and the most to do, stole down the dark corridor and out into the equally black street. Behind him the others would come, one at a time, to find their positions and begin their own tasks. He had almost forgotten the Skerl. The brush of spiky fur against his ankle startled him for an instant, and he bent to put a hand on its small head. The chilly nose bumped deliberately into his palm, as if reassuring him. Once he straightened and headed for his goal, he knew the creature would be with him to the end.

As he waited for the night, he had recalled every step of the way he must go, each door, lane, gate, and cranny that led into the Elector's house. In the intervening years, some of the entries might well have been stopped up by some guard who remembered or discovered them, but there had been so many secret bolt-holes he was certain no one would have found them all. So far as he knew, only he and his comrade of long ago had ever so much as explored them.

Forgotten alleyways led to storage bins for fuel, foodstuffs, fodder, and wine. Some of those bins had probably been moved to more convenient locations, the alleys leading to them barred and the doors entering them locked. But once there had been stables in the middle of the vast pile, with their own concealed exits, so secret and labyrinthine it made one wonder on what errands long-ago horsemen might have been sent in the night.

He had, in the past, found many cracks that had been caused by settling of the heavy masonry. There would probably be more now, after so many years. But before trying such difficult ways, he was heading first for one of the old stable-runs. That would be made to his order, if it still existed.

He found he needed little light. His feet seemed to remember their path over the gravel-stone streets, without consulting his conscious memory. He made one false turn, but the Skerl, as if knowing his destination, nudged him gently into the right course again.

Just as the Shepherd's Crook rose in the east above the row of roofs, he found the pillar with the head of a horse carved into its top. He paused there to listen. A fountain trickled softly beyond the wall to his right—that told him he was in the right place, for he remembered the soft sound from his early exploration.

He turned to the left and headed around the block that was the Elector's vast house. It was very dark, for the Elector did not set lanterns along the streets beside his dwelling. Lehnik could hear the grate of watchmen's boots on the other side of the wall along which he walked, but at last he moved into a tangle of doorways, grated gates, and scarred stone walls running along the back alleys serving the House.

He ran his hand along the wall, feeling a flower cut into the dry old wood of a door. That was one of his old check-points. He counted the sequence off again, to make sure. The pillar. The cracked wall. The notch. The door. At last he stood where he wanted to be.

This wall seemed to stand flush with the rest of the block, but he knew of old that it held a concealed setback. The entrance was hard to find, even by day, but to his astonishment he found it more easily in the dark, when his eye was not fooled by the architectural disguises designed to conceal it.

His hand touched the grillwork he remembered, rusty, dampish and scaly to his touch. The lock, now—he felt along the ironwork gate—had crumbled with time and now hung useless from its rust-eaten chain.

Lehnik shook his head. He would climb over it, for any movement of that ancient metal would squeal like tortured cats, he felt certain. It shook beneath his weight, but he went up fast and leaped clear from its top.

His soft boots met the stone with a muffled thud, and he stood for a long moment, listening hard. Only the *fuf-fuf* of the Skerl's pads on the pavement came to his ears.

The great House seemed to sleep deeply, though Lehnik knew night-guards walked there, advisors plotted, entertainers and courtesans paraded, yawning, in the inhabited parts of the complex. These were the old, ruinous areas of the place, just suited to his needs.

He followed the alley, which was just wide enough to allow a ridden horse to pass. Even then, the knees of any rider must have bumped on the stony walls on both sides.

The strip of stars above the alley disappeared as an arch of masonry intervened. He was now at the point where the passage dived beneath the House itself. There should be, he recalled, a decorated lintel here. His hand found it and moved across it. His memory had served him faultlessly, so far.

His quiet footfalls whispered along the tunnel that he entered. Lehnik lightened his step, listening tensely until only the shadow of an echo followed him as he moved. His hand found another door, just where it should be. An abrupt bend to the right took him between the walls of apartments which must not have been used in generations, and then there was a hint of light: starlight, brilliant after the intense darkness of the tunnel.

The tiny court upon which the stables faced was before him. A hiss from the dimness brought him up short. "Brother!" said a gruff voice. "You are very early."

The tone was familiar, even used so softly. It sounded like that Brother who had overseen his entry into the Armory. Was he a conspirator to something that was secret even from the Elector?

Lehnik, trained in the harshest of schools, did not hesitate. The fate of his country and his world lay in his hands.

He leaped across the distance between that voice and himself, and his hands closed about the stalk-like neck of the Teacher of the Spirit. There was a gasp of terror and surprise just before he tightened his grip and a grinding click told him the neck had broken. The twitching man hung from his fingers.

Now he faced a dilemma. Someone else was expected to come in this direction, and very soon. He didn't have a way of knowing how early he might be or how well his victim judged the expected visitor's arrival. He must get himself and the dead man out of sight at once.

The Brother had been waiting outside a door, which was probably the one through which he had entered the court. To use that one would be more than foolish. Probably other Brothers waited there for their guest.

No, he must go somewhere else, very quickly.

Though not overlarge, Lehnik had that strength that people who are wiry and tough can develop over the years. The Brother, though much taller, was so skinny his weight was manageable.

Lehnik tied the limp body to his back with straps from his pack. Then he moved to the wall opposite the doorway and felt along its surface. There was the stonework he had admired, in that long-ago past when he first discovered this stable. Cut deeply into the stone of the wall in herringbone design, it was interlaced with a pattern of twisting vines. At that moment, his mind charged with his need, Lehnik felt he could have drawn it from memory.

Balancing his awkward burden, he reached up to find a hand-hold, set his foot into the lowest of the designs, and took a step upward. There he found another handhold. The dead weight of the Brother threatened to pull him backward off the wall, as if the fellow tried to avenge himself even after dying, but he struggled upward stubbornly.

There was a place where the overhang of the stable roofs met the wall. Made of shingled wood, they were probably treacherously rotted by now, but this would have to do. There Lehnik paused to listen.

There had been the echo of a step in the tunnel he had left behind. The visitor must be coming, right now.

Lehnik laid the dead man flat against the wall, in the angle where it met the roof. Though the shingles sagged beneath the weight, the thing held. He lay beside the corpse, motionless, almost breathless.

The visitor came confidently, without any attempt at secrecy, so hidden and uninhabited was this area of the House. His husky voice called, "Brother? Brother? Are you here?" He sounded a bit angry when there was no answer.

"Brother, I was told you would be waiting for me!" He paused, waiting for a reply that did not come.

Lehnik knew surely that in a moment those inside would realize something had happened to their companion. They would search, probably with torches. He made sure his victim was pushed tightly against the wall, invisible from below. Then he hooked his wiry fingers into the stonework and climbed swiftly up the sheer face of stone looming over the stable.

153

He left the ominous courtyard behind him and sighed with relief. As he reached the topmost roof, he heard a door open below. Voices murmured, rising to a sharp exclamation.

Lehnik stepped softly onto the cornice, gave a slight heave, and was on the rooftop. He dropped flat on his stomach and lay, eyes level with the edge of the wall. Whatever happened below, he wanted to know about it, for this conspiracy of Brothers might have a bearing on the problems facing his own people.

A big fellow in the gray of the Brothers' garb brought a torch into the stable yard. He bent to stare at the stone paving, and while he checked it, another came with another torch and went into the tunnel. Soon they were studying every inch of the area, but no one called aloud or spoke above a murmur.

The big Brother moved into the abandoned stable. His light flashed in winks as he passed from stall to stall, and Lehnik was glad he had abandoned his impulse to hide himself and his victim there.

The newcomer went in at the door. Only the two searchers were left outside, and Lehnik gave up any hope that he might learn anything useful. He inched back from the edge.

He now knew where he was, within a few dozen yards, for he could see against the stars another dark square, jutting above this level of roof at some distance to his right. A balcony there marked a black slash across the sky. That was another of the sets of rooms, one of which he and his companion had occupied many years before.

He climbed to reach the balcony, and went silently to find a door leading into the dusty, cobwebby apartment. He sighed with relief. One part of his task had been made easier.

That left another, all but impossible. He had to find a way to accomplish it, before he was through.

CHAPTER TWENTY

Lehnik suddenly remembered the Skerl. Had the small creature managed to make the steep climb? He'd been too busy to think about it until now. He felt around with his foot, but no spike-furred shape could he find at his ankles. He didn't dare call.

He sighed. Perhaps if he went back out onto the balcony...but at that point a flutter touched his mind, something like that he felt from the Sisters, but fainter, slightly alien in feel. The Skerl was somewhere within range. Could it follow his mind-pattern from a distance?

Now his eyes were adjusting to the dimness, for the starlight was considerable and there were no intervening walls or structures at this height to block it. He could see dark bulks of dust-shrouded furniture in the room. He would have to move carefully, for in the night a thump as he knocked something over would be all too audible, even several floors below.

As he felt his way, he heard the *fuf-fuf* of the Skerl's paws. The sound was coming toward him from the direction in which he was headed. How had the creature known where to come after him?

Then he remembered that Sallek said the Skerl had been prowling about in the Elector's house for days, now. Being small and unobtrusive, it could go where he could not, back in his youth. Undistinguishable from the pet Skerl of the household, it should have been able to explore every part of the vast complex.

Its nose touched his leg. He leaned to set his fingers on its head, and it turned to lead him out of the room into the corridor.

The hallway was as dark as the tunnel he had left below, but he thought he remembered the direction in which the attics lay. As he thought it would, a door at the end of the hallway opened onto a narrow stair leading straight up. Lehnik muffled a sneeze, heard a choking cough from the Skerl, and started up the sagging, cobweb-hung stairway.

155

After a fairly long climb, this led onto an open colonnade, which formed a balcony for the apartments it served as a corridor. He was now very high, and the night breeze was cool as he felt his way along.

Then the night exploded into chaos, wild noise, shouts, screams. *Tat-tat-tat-pow!* There were stuttering explosions, and sparks of light shot up from the dark street beyond the distant wall of the House.

Men came dashing out of the Armory, just visible beyond the roofs and the surrounding wall. They carried torches, and he knew they were armed, ready for battle, and that they would only stand in the street, bewildered, when they arrived amid the scene taking place there.

Lehnik grinned. Benthe and Speaker's gifts were making a more than adequate diversion. He knew guards from the Elector's house would gather at the gates, trying to learn if the noise posed any threat to their charge. Probably many of those living in the palace would hurry there, too, clad in bed gowns and anxious to know what was happening.

He felt along the wall. Ten arches he had already passed. There should be a door—here!

There was. The Skerl moved against his leg, pushing into the opening ahead of him, and he heard its scrabbling paws as it passed through invisible chambers that were wells of air no man had breathed in many years.

He heard mice scurry, felt the filaments of spider web against his face until he was veiled once again. But he was almost there, he knew.

The last door opened onto the corridor he remembered. At the farther end, some yards from his present position, it gave onto the room he had shared with his young comrade in the old days, while at this end it gave onto the section of roof he had wanted to find.

Once he was again in the open, he found the starlight perfectly adequate. Seven stacks over, fifteen to the west; he counted carefully.

There, looming against the sky, was the great air vent he had sought. It stood less than his own height above the roof-top, for it did not carry away smoke but only provided ventilation to those below. In a moment, he was inside the thing, finding the stone rungs he had used before cut into the masonry. Those were designed, he was sure, to give cleaners access to the length of the thing.

It was a very long way to the bottom, and he passed through all the layers of the House, into the bed-rock beneath it. There were gratings through which he could hear stirrings and words and occasional quarrels among those living in the rooms the vents served. He thought, on that long descent, that the Elector would shiver in his bones if he knew how easily one of his enemies had gained access to his house.

The Skerl, using some means best known to it, was climbing down after him, dislodging particles from the stonework above his head. He found himself glad of the creature's company. If something broke and let him fall to the bottom of the shaft, he would lie there, dying or dead. His flesh would rot, and no one would ever know where he lay, if the Skerl did not carry the news back to his people.

His foot reached for a step at last and found a flagged floor instead. It had seemed to take forever, but at last he was at the bottom of the shaft.

He laid his hands on the wall and felt all the way around. The last time he had stood in that place there had been a torch standard that held the remnant of a torch, and if he were lucky nobody would have bothered to clean the shaft in all those years. The thing might still be there.

Instead, there was a metal basket on a shelf, holding candles. Indeed, he found other shelves that held a variety of supplies and cleaning equipment. Evidently, those who worked in these deep places found the end of the shaft a convenient storage closet.

With great satisfaction, Lehnik secured several candles and managed to light one, using the flint and steel he always carried in a pocket to kindle a bit of fluff from his cloak. When the tiny flame had caught the wick, he held up the light and stared about.

He stood in the bottom of the shaft, which here was a sort of niche in the wall. He stepped out into an inky space and saw passages extending to left and right. Cells faced this narrow corridor, their metalwork glinting dully in the candlelight.

The cells were, of course, empty. Even if the Elector had kept prisoners here, he would hardly have left them in the same place as his newly acquired weapons.

He thought for a moment. For convenience, the things should be stored in the cells nearest the great door that had replaced the iron-studded wooden one he had seen before. The heavy thing shone lead-gray in his feeble light. Wood sheathed in lead, he thought, had formed it, or it would have been entirely too heavy for the hinges to hold up.

He moved silently along the line of cells, noting the scuffling of dust caused by those bringing in the bales and crates he could now see bulking darkly behind the barred grillwork. The first cell near the door was filled with those, barrels, bundles, long rolls.

Lehnik sniffed. An oily, metallic smell lay on the dank air. There was also a hint of something else, alien and disturbing. He had never smelled anything like it before.

To his amusement, the cell was locked, as if the objects imprisoned there might try to escape. His lip curled. There spoke the military mind, invariably suspicious. He suspected it might take three officers with three different keys to open the leaden door, and another trio to open the cell.

A troop of guards was on duty outside at all times, too. He almost laughed. One would think a dangerous maniac was secured inside the cell instead of outside, in the House of the Elector.

He had no need for entering the cell. He had, indeed, no desire to make any closer acquaintance with those weapons. Instead, he knelt and pressed his knee down onto the egg-shape that Benthe had given him. With his thumb he pushed in the button, requiring most of his strength to manage it. The device had not been designed to work accidentally, it was obvious.

The button moved at last, slowly, into the egg. At last its entire length was countersunk into the thing, and Lehnik found he was panting.

He paused and breathed deeply, controlling his reactions. Then he rolled the ovoid into the cell. It went easily between the bars and nestled at the curve of a barrel, held by the end of a roll.

He expelled his lungful of air; then he exploded into motion. Lehnik shot toward the chimney, where he set the candle, blown out by the wind of his passing, in the box and began climbing. His weary legs felt as if they would buckle under his weight as the Skerl scrabbled ahead of him. The slight patter of grit on his head was no bother at all.

He looked up frequently at the patch of stars at the mouth of the vent; it grew larger and larger, and at last he crawled out onto the tiled roof. He lay flat, panting for breath. He had never moved so fast, and now his legs felt watery.

Benthe had said he should have half an hour after the beginning of the diversion. He had been at least half of that climbing down the stack and doing what was necessary. Fast as he came, some time had been required to make the climb back up. He had better move fast, no matter how hard his heart was pounding.

Groaning quietly, he rolled onto his stomach and lifted himself onto hands and knees, moving toward the window from which he had dropped onto the roof. It was a terrible effort to pull himself up and in, but he managed it. Then, come what might, he knew that he must rest.

The Skerl curled into his lap as he leaned against a wall, his legs crossed, his head back. Even as he gasped for breath, there came a quiet quiver from someplace deep below the apartments where they sat. Ancient stones grated subtly, and somewhere something cracked sharply. Plaster drifted down like snow onto Lehnik's skin.

He straightened, listening hard. Had anyone else noticed that shifting, or had Benthe's diversion distracted them too much for it to catch the attention of those on guard?

Very distantly, there came another sound, a muffled *crrrrump!* Was that the wall of the prison block? Was the Sister even now being found and carried away? He hoped that might be true.

As for escaping, himself, he knew he could not go back by the way he had come. The Brothers would be buzzing like disturbed bees in that lost courtyard all this night and for some time to come. He had to take another route, but now he was too weary to recall the way.

His mind seemed filled with mud, and his thoughts slid away when he tried to catch them. He jerked himself back from the edge of sleep, his head coming up again reluctantly.

The Skerl was up now, tugging at his boot with its tiny teeth. Of course. It knew all the ways. Why had he not remembered that?

Lehnik knew he was unfit for more climbing, up or down. The way he took must be easy, or he would never make it. His wound, though it was healed, was making itself felt very sharply, and he understood he had not replaced the strength he used in healing it. When he needed more energy, it simply was not there.

The small creature sped ahead of him, down the hall to the main stairway. He thudded down the steps, only his trained will keeping him moving.

After some time they found themselves down on a tenanted level. He came out of the door concealing the back-stair and found a pert-eyed maid eyeing him. But he managed to move normally down the hall to the next flight of stairs. He tried to smile as he passed her, while he blessed his guard's uniform.

"Drunken soldiers!" he heard her say behind him. "All over the place! It's enough to make you sick."

Then he understood what the Skerl was doing, and that amused him. They would pass through the House as one of its own, unchallenged and unnoticed. He hadn't the energy left to chuckle, as he followed his small guide down stair after stair, hallway after hallway.

At last he found himself in the main hall, remembered from earlier visits. It was buzzing with disturbed people.

Gorst himself was directing groups of guardsmen. Lehnik found himself grateful that he had known the big officer only by reputation instead of in person.

A sergeant caught Lehnik by the elbow. "Why aren't you on duty? We have an emergency here!" he snapped. Then he looked closely at the soldier he had collared and stepped back. "Disgraceful! Dirty and drunk—get yourself together, or I'll put you on report!"

"Yessir," Lehnik gulped, trying to sound as intoxicated as possible.

He staggered on, ignored by the busy troops about him. Those noticing his passing had no time to bother with him, so he swayed to the small side door and leered at the guard on duty there.

"Mo'...*hic*...more wine," he said, grinning.

The guard looked disgusted. "You go out and get some fresh air, so you'll be some good to us. We have no time for your kind, now."

Lehnik stumbled past him and down the short flight of steps into the garden. Once at the bottom, he grabbed his gut and ran for the shrubbery, as if to vomit. Nobody paid any attention to him, as far as he could tell.

Slithering through the greenery, he found himself feeling better, getting a second wind of sorts. Did the Sisters need help? he wondered. He almost headed in that direction, but better judgment overruled the impulse.

They were as capable of doing their job as he was. He would go back to Shira's house, as they had agreed. He looked about for the Skerl, but it was gone. Probably to help Sallek and her people, he felt, though he could not be certain of that.

It took some time to reach Shira's house, for his limbs simply would not move quickly. At last he touched the door he had left hours before, and it opened. He stumbled into the hallway, where a hand caught his and led him to the door of the windowless room.

There was a scritch, and the lamp lit. He stood stupidly, staring about him. Benthe was there, safe and sound. Shira, too, and Elie, though he wondered if they had waited quietly as they had been told to. Something about the attitudes of all three spoke of strain.

"Kerrill?" he asked, while they helped him onto a mat and offered him water. "Sallek? The little one with no name?"

"They'll come," Benthe growled. "What about the weapons?"

"If the device worked, which I think it must have from the vibrations I felt, they are all gone. The Elector doesn't know it and won't until someone goes into the Keep to check.

"But what about the others? The Sister...." His voice trailed off.

They smiled at him confidently, but something in their eyes told him they were worried, as well.

CHAPTER TWENTY-ONE

As he waited, Lehnik slipped into that white space inside, feeling grateful for his training that allowed him to take refuge there. But even then a faint unease touched him, for he had been too fortunate in his own efforts. Surely the others could not have been so lucky.

Their task had exposed them to guards and street people. They were exposed, vulnerable—he tried to prepare himself for losing any of their number, but a strange question came suddenly to mind, sending his thoughts in a different direction.

He had been lying on his pallet in darkness, and now he asked of his unseen comrades, "Is there any teaching among the Sisters of Silence or even the Brotherhood about all the different races living on our world? Speaker said something once that interested me, and I have puzzled over it since. It just came to mind."

Benthe's voice came out of the darkness. "The Brothers have much to say on the subject, as on most. They dislike any crossing of lines of color in marriage, as in many other things. I have often thought that they try to divide people along any lines possible, man from woman, black from white from tan."

"Ah." Lehnik closed his eyes again, feeling this was something he should have guessed. His mind had been working quietly on that puzzle while the rest of him was otherwise occupied, and this last bit made it all come into focus as a logical pattern.

Divisions among people make for friction. They foment quarrels and sometimes wars. In the midst of such upsets men who need power tend to reach out for control over others. The Teachers of the Spirit were evidently corrupted now, driving wedges between men and nations where they found it possible.

Satisfied with his answer, he allowed himself to relax, waiting again in silence. The dark hours passed, and slowly Lehnik felt his strength returning. Yet he also felt a subtle difference inside. Something had changed, though he refused to allow that to trouble him.

162

At last there was a sound in the corridor. Shira, who had been watching at the outer door, called softly, "They are here!"

Lehnik came to his feet, fumbling for the lamp and the coal-pot used to kindle it. As the warm light blossomed from the wick, three shapes clad in soldier-green stumbled into the room. The larger of the two carried a limp body in his arms.

"Kerrill!" Lehnik took the Sister from him and laid her gently onto his own mat. He touched Sallek's cheek and said, "Sister Elie, the box of medications. She has blood on her uniform."

The nameless Sister sank wearily onto a stool, and he saw her face was streaked with bloody traces that oozed down from a cut at her hairline. She held her left arm and shoulder stiffly, as if they were painful.

Elie came at once and knelt to sponge away the blood from the rescued Sister's skin. Satisfied that she was being tended, Lehnik turned to the nameless Sister, who smiled into his face and crumpled into a heap at his feet.

He went to his knees beside her and felt for her pulse. He could see no open wound, but he felt at her neck, and there was no heart-beat there. She was dead.

He slipped his hand from beneath her and eased her down. Her cloak slipped aside, and he felt a patch of stickiness. There was a long sliver of wood embedded in her side, surrounded by small cir-cle of blood.

Kerrill had knelt on the other side of their Sister. He reached a gentle hand to close her blank eyes. "The explosion must have sent that through her. All the while we worked, she was bleeding to death inside." His voice died, and he scrubbed at his eyes like a small boy.

Shira had been helping Elie with Sallek, but now she came to touch the colorless forehead of her old companion. "Oh, Sister! Sister! I was afraid it would come to this," she murmured.

Recalling that Shira and this Sister had been members of the same House, here in Garrouche, Lehnik asked her, "Did you know her name? I never heard it, and she was someone who should be re-membered."

Shira jerked the soldier's cap from her friend's head, and her eyes filled with tears. "We were friends as much as Sisters can be, when they are always sent to different places on different errands. We trained together and grew to love and respect each other.

"She did have a name, but only I and our Speaker knew it. She would not use the one with which she was born, and she refused to accept a false one, preferring to remain nameless."

She stared down at the still body. "She was the Elector's daughter. Her mother died when she was small, and she learned her father's true nature when she was still almost an infant. She came to our House when she was ten, insisting this was what she wanted to do. She never saw him again."

Lehnik felt terrible pity for this one, caught between family and her own sense of right. But Sallek was continuing, "She was ashamed of the things he caused to be done, both to his own citizens and their neighbors. When he captured our Sister and found the way to breach our House, she was devastated, feeling in some way it must be her fault, that her presence had triggered his attack."

She drew a deep breath and straightened her shoulders, turning back to the Sister they had saved from captivity. Lehnik bent over that white-clad shape, able to see only the forehead and eyelids. To his surprise, the skin was as black as Speaker's, smooth and youthful.

Shira lifted the dirty white sleeve and touched puckered marks that showed faintly pink against the dark skin. Something had been injected into the woman's body that took control of her and forced her to do things totally against her will and her training.

"The Stronghold will buzz with activity, after losing this one," Benthe said. He was speaking as if to himself, but he went on, "It will be hard for us to get out of the walls, for a long while."

"There is no hurry." Shira had returned to the use of hand-signs, once the dead Sister was covered over. "This house will not be searched, for no one has lived here for many years. The servant who comes to clean and air it is not due for some days, but I can use my disguise to go and come in her place. I can bring food and news from the market."

Kerrill was binding Sallek's head now, so he spoke aloud. "We need rest. Our wounded need time to heal, for even with concentration that takes some time, as well as nutritious food." He tied off the head-band and gestured toward the still shape beneath the blanket.

"What of her body? It is spring, getting warmer every day. I would not put her away like a dead animal, for she deserves every honor."

Shira thought for a moment. "There is a tiny garden enclosed in the center of this house. No other overlooks it, and she can go there, beneath my mother's rose tree. Her garment of flesh can rest there, while her spirit goes away to the white spaces."

With little fuss, the grave was dug and the small body placed in it, wrapped in rich rugs from unused rooms in the house. Then they rested, and the warm days, in addition to the fresh food Shira brought from the market, put strength into them all.

In less than a week, the Sister they had rescued woke from the coma in which she had lain and looked about. Shira had dressed her in a white gown that had belonged to her mother, replacing the draggled robes she had worn for so long. She looked around at the soiled soldier-garb worn by the others.

Her dark hands moved, twitching her sleeves away from her hands. Agate eyes regarded her forearms, which now were healing but still showed the marks of needles. She looked up at Kerrill and Lehnik, bewildered.

Kerrill motioned, "You are among Sisters. We are disguised for safety's sake, but we took you from the prison."

The big eyes widened, and the hands moved again. "I am grateful, but they will find and kill you."

Lehnik stooped to take her hands, smoothing them to stillness. Then he loosed her and spoke his own hand-sign. "We are well hidden, and we have destroyed the weapons that were in your House. The Elector has other things to think about now, for his troops are returning from Trans-Kell. We can see them moving, from the top of this house, and they seem terribly dispirited.

"Without those weapons, the invasion cannot succeed for very long. Trans-Kell has had time to organize its defense. Krohm is a better strategist than Gorst, and the outcome will never be in doubt if their forces meet head to head. Those are not victorious troops we watch from the roof."

* * * * * * *

Within a week, she was able to go to the rooftop and see for herself. All the Sisters could stare over the wall and most of the intervening houses to see the road that led, in the end, to Kell-Ford. Wagons of wounded toiled up to the gates, and those fresh soldiers who had roamed the streets of the Stronghold were gone, chewed up in the jaws of war. Those who returned looked defeated and exhausted.

Lehnik knew that before long his people could leave the city without a question being asked or anyone showing interest. They had only to wait a few days more.

Each Sister came to have a favorite spot in the huge house. Sallek lived in the library, poring over big volumes of history and natural science.

Kerrill loved the rooftop, which gave a counterfeit of freedom, Benthe liked the kitchen, where he showed a surprising aptitude for cookery.

Shira and Sister Clee preferred the small garden where the Elector's daughter had found peace. The rose-tree was in bud, and they would sit there in silence, their fingers sometimes busy, sometimes folded in their laps in the spring sun.

One evening Lehnik found Shira there, when he came down from the roof and wandered into the garden. He and Kerrill had been keeping watch on the city, checking for a quiet time when the group could make their way out of the city.

"Krohm is coming," he said. "The banner of Trans-Kell heads the formation of horsemen coming up the road. I dare to hope this war is over."

"Or a siege begun?" Shira's fingers asked.

"The gates are open," he signed. "The Elector's coach sped away two hours ago in a cloud of dust. I think this particular conflict is done with."

She sighed. Sister Clee stood and moved toward the door, turning to sign, "I will go and watch. Though I was helpless against their drugs, I will always feel guilty at the trouble my weakness has caused."

Shira smiled sadly. "She will, of course. A pity, for of all concerned, only the Elector and his advisers and the Brotherhood seem to be fully culpable. I suspect, indeed, that the Teachers of the Spirit are more guilty than most."

Lehnik wasn't listening, for he watched her eyes, dark above the veiling she had made from linens belonging to the house. From that core of balance he had found inside, he reached out to her. His fingers moved, and her gaze dropped to watch his hands.

"In time, when we grow weary and have done our best for the Order, will you share our older years with me?" his calloused fingers asked. "Perhaps Cylla will be our child, and her children our grandchildren."

The black eyes smiled above the white veil. Her hand reached to still his. The veil moved with her words.

"Yes," she said. "When the time comes, yes."

Their hands clasped together. Lehnik found his spirit lifting. Wherever they were sent, whatever task either was assigned, they would know that in time to come they would know peace and companionship.

Her thought fluttered at the edge of his mind, and he sighed. Perhaps in time he might even find the ability to link with her thoughts.

Benthe pounded into the room. "I'm going out to find Krohm. The army is inside the walls, now," he gestured.

Lehnik looked after him. Then he turned again to Shira. "Are there any more spare sheets?" he asked with his hands.

She nodded.

"Then we'd better make fresh robes and veils for us all, except for Benthe. It wouldn't be wise to unsettle the army in its moment of triumph. More than one of those who is coming has served with me and would know me. That would shake their faith in the Sisterhood, if they knew you took in rogues like me."

She laughed and hurried away after the linens. Lehnik almost spoke aloud, but then he closed his lips. Once more the world would become totally wordless, filled with a cleanliness he had not found anywhere else in his troubled world.

He would speak again with Speaker, when they returned to the House in Trans-Kell, but not for years would he speak again to Shira, or she to him.

There was no need. They were both Sisters.

www.ingramcontent.com/pod-product-compliance
Lightning Source LLC
Chambersburg PA
CBHW020644180626
46816CB00003B/1123